WHAT WE FED TO THE MANTICORE

TALIA LAKSHMI KOLLURI

 TIN HOUSE / Portland, Oregon

WHAT WE FED TO THE MANTICORE

Published by Tin House, Portland, Oregon

Distributed by W. W. Norton & Company

Library of Congress Cataloging-in-Publication Data

Names: Kolluri, Talia Lakshmi, 1979- author.
Title: What we fed to the manticore / Talia Lakshmi Kolluri.
Other titles: What we fed to the manticore (Compilation)
Description: Portland, Oregon : Tin House, [2022] | Includes
    bibliographical references.
Identifiers: LCCN 2022014548 | ISBN 9781953534415 (paperback) |
    ISBN 9781953534491 (ebook)
Subjects: LCSH: Animals—Fiction. | LCGFT: Animal fiction. |
    Short stories.
Classification: LCC PS3611.O55 W48 2022 | DDC 813/.6—dc23/
    eng/20220407
LC record available at https://lccn.loc.gov/2022014548

First US Edition 2022
Printed in the USA
Interior design by Jakob Vala

www.tinhouse.com

CONTENTS

For Jared, who is a little bit wild.
And for Lulu, who made me a little bit tame.

THE GOOD DONKEY

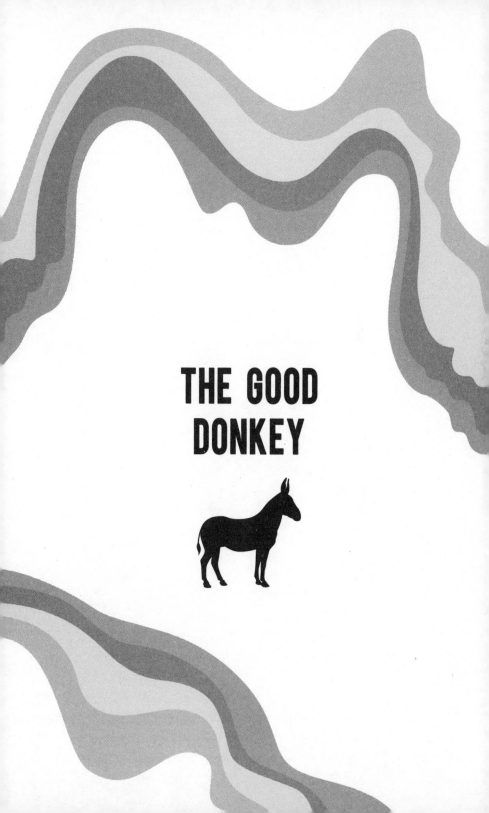

I am not pleased. Paint is dripping down my hoof and the colors are muddled together. I shouldn't complain. I agreed to it, of course.

Hafiz is putting together a zoo. And he asked me to be the zebra.

"You're a very good donkey, habibi," he told me three days ago, "but the border is closed, and everyone says prices for using the smuggling tunnels have gone up. I can't afford the zebra in Damascus, and the one in Cairo is twice that price." He gestured wildly, scattering my oats. What a waste.

I don't know much about borders, but I would do anything for Hafiz. He is more than a father to me.

And so here I am, Hafiz painting me in black and white stripes. He has hung two torches from the ceiling with strings, to use when the power is cut, and the one above me swings gently, pitching its light back and forth and making me dizzy. Hafiz has stopped in the middle, and knowing him, the paint will dry unevenly and I will look awful. And then what kind of zebra will I be?

We are in my little stable behind the house when the knocking starts. The door is flimsy. The building is flimsy. And so

3

things around us tremble when anyone raps on it. He should be paying attention to me and to what he is doing, but he goes anyway. It's always like this with Hafiz and me. I am here. He goes. There is always someone else. He returns. And I am still here.

This time he returns with several men I don't recognize. They're gathered in clusters, some with their backs to me. They speak in low voices, and every so often one of them grunts as though he is carrying something heavy.

"This is the man I was telling you about," says one of the strangers.

"Masha'Allah, it's good that you are here and willing to take them in," says another to Hafiz.

"Yes, yes, of course, bring them in." Hafiz opens the doors wide. "Alhamdulillah. They are alive; that's all that matters."

"Where do you want them?" asks another stranger. This one sounds angry. Or irritated. They all struggle through the main area of my stable, as though they aren't used to carrying things.

"Over here. Here by my . . . over here." Hafiz has led them to me. There is a bed of hay that I like to lie on, and Hafiz has brought them to it. He isn't sure what to call me at this precise moment. I am half done and dripping paint. I try to catch his eye so I can stare at him pointedly, but he's busy smoothing the hay—my hay—into a round and even mound.

I don't like the way these strangers smell. Sweaty, and a little like gasoline. They crowd near me with two large bundles, several men to each bundle.

"Are they sedated?" Hafiz asks.

"Yes," says the first man. He must be the leader, because he isn't carrying anything. "For the journey. Also, they are tame.

4

They've been hand-raised since birth. Like house cats." The leader puts his hands on his hips as he watches the others, and smiles widely.

"Have they been in a zoo before?" Hafiz stands with the leader and watches the others lay two enormous, rough cloth bundles on my hay. He runs a hand over his beard, in the same measured rhythm he uses when he brushes me.

"Yes, yes. They were in a little zoo in Beit Hanoun," the leader says. "The zoo was lucky to have them, you know." Hafiz nods. I walk closer to him and stand at his shoulder. Hafiz reaches back and starts to scratch my chin. We both watch the bundles as they start moving. I smell something musky. Familiar, but I can't place it.

"The female was stolen." The leader reaches into his pocket and pulls out a packet of cigarettes. Hafiz watches warily as the man lights one and gestures toward one of the bundles with the lit end. "She was missing for three months. We found her with a bunch of bandits. They were charging families to take photos with her. But, you know, they mistreated her, so she's skittish.

"Actually, they're both that way now," the leader goes on. "It was the airstrikes. They hit part of the zoo and much of the grounds were destroyed.

"You know," he starts up again, tapping ash off his cigarette, "I was surprised to hear there was a zoo in Gaza City. I thought it closed."

"It did," says Hafiz. "I'm reopening it on the old site. It's just down the road. I used to take my nieces there." Hafiz glances back at me and then turns to the leader. "Children are still children, you know. Even in times like this."

The leader nods at Hafiz, times like this being what they are. "I went there, you know," he says. "To the university. The one south of the zoo."

"Oh?"

"Yes, three semesters."

"What did you study?" Hafiz scratches his nose and looks around. He never went to university, which is fine with me.

"Philosophy," says the leader, laughing, "which disappointed my father. He wanted me to be an accountant."

"And you didn't finish?"

"No," a pause while the leader smokes, "but, you know, now I do this." He reaches his hand out in a sweeping motion to take in my stable and me, as if we make up the whole of his life.

"And what does your father think of that?" Hafiz asks.

"My father is dead." Hafiz and the leader stare at each other until Hafiz looks down. "Come, let me tell you what I know about how to take care of them." The leader puts a hand on Hafiz's shoulder and leads him away from me.

Eventually, the strangers all leave. Hafiz absentmindedly pats my flank and then goes back to his own house, and I'm left here to figure this out by myself. The two bundles take up every inch of space on my hay. Where am I supposed to go now?

I stare at the two of them. One of them is moving more, and a gap in the fabric has started to pull apart. A large, tawny-haired paw emerges with dusty black pads on the bottom. The paw swipes at the fabric, pulls it away, and reveals an unmistakable head.

He blinks warily, yawns widely, and then pulls at the fabric enfolding his companion. Another head appears, and they both fully emerge, stretching lazily and kicking the rest of the fabric away to reveal the full length of themselves.

The male has a mane, so he's grown, but the mane looks shabby. He's emaciated. They both are, actually.

"What are you supposed to be?" asks the male.

"I'm a zebra," I say. I stand up a little straighter, stretching my neck out as long as I can. I flick my tail a couple of times. I don't know them, and honestly this is none of their business.

"I don't think that's true," says the male.

"Are you calling me a liar?" I ask.

"He didn't finish you," says the female. She is so quiet I can barely hear her, but she is loud enough for me to know I'm being insulted. "Your face is convincing enough. He did a nice job, but your back end isn't done. I can see it. And it's dripped onto your hoof."

"Yes, I know." I look down and see that the tear of white paint that had run earlier has dried. I knew it would be this way.

Hafiz. He forgot about me.

"It doesn't matter," I say loudly. "What's important is that when Hafiz is done, the children won't know the difference. They will be happy anyway. And that's what's important, you know. The *children*."

I haven't seen any lions in years. I wouldn't say that I've missed them.

Hafiz is late with my breakfast. When he finally comes in, he is carrying a bunch of oats under one arm and struggling to carry a bucket full of soapy water and a brush with the other. A bag is slung over his shoulder and a towel hangs around his neck.

"We have to wash all that off and start over," he says without even greeting me.

"Hello," I say.

"Yes, yes, hello, yes. Hurry up and eat. I need the paint to dry before I take you and your things over."

"Over where?" I didn't sleep well. Those lions were snoring. And I didn't like looking at them when they came in. I didn't like seeing all their bones jutting out everywhere. It wasn't nice. Hafiz wets the brush and swoops it down my flank in long strokes.

"The zoo. To the zoo, you idiot. Have you forgotten? You're the zebra." He puts the brush down and reaches into his bag.

"Right, right." I remember. Hafiz offers me a carrot. When I pick it up, I let my lips brush his flat palm. He said once that he liked that. I like carrots. They're sweet, and I like the texture. So crunchy. We don't have them very often. It's a treat. I must have been good. I know I'm the only one he has, but I really am a very good donkey for Hafiz. I'm an excellent donkey. I'm sure I'll make a very fine zebra. I'll do my best. I think if I concentrate on the thought of a zebra in my mind, I'll be able to feel it in my body. *Become* a zebra. I think. . . . "Wait, Hafiz?"

"Yes?" He moves the brush up to my neck and sweeps down to my shoulders. I like the feel of the bristles. They get just past my coat, and I can feel them on my skin. I could fall asleep like this.

"My things. Why are we taking my things?"

Hafiz stops with the brush and walks to my face. He holds it in his hands and presses his forehead against mine. "You have to stay there, habibi. That's how it works."

"Stay? But only during the day, yes? When the children are there?"

"At night too," he says, and goes back to sweeping the brush across my flank. I look down at my front feet and see a soapy gray mess has pooled in the dirt. This is turning my floor into mud. I don't like it.

"But I live here," I say quietly. "I live here with you."

"Think of the others." He puts the brush down and picks up the towel. He dries me swiftly, as though there is no time to waste. "What would they think if I treated you differently? If I treat you like you are special, then it might make them feel bad, yes?"

"But I am special," I say, mostly to myself. Hafiz laughs, and now I'm embarrassed. I don't like when he laughs at me. I'm not meant to be funny. It reminds me of when I was smaller and wasn't used to the length of my legs, or the time when he put that bow on my tail and all the goats said I was his girlfriend. I remember yelling at them, *He's going to eat you all!* "I AM SPECIAL!" I bray, much louder than I intend. I don't like my voice when it's loud. To me it sounds like unrestrained honking, and nobody takes me seriously when I do it.

"Of course, habibi. Very special." I can hear his words spread out the way they do when he's smiling, as he picks up his jars of white and black paint. Of course I am a joke to him. Let him see me stop carrying things, and then he will know.

9

Hafiz walks me to the zoo. It's a short distance down the road from the small plot of land where he keeps my stable and where we have always lived. The sign for the zoo is actually remade from the old sign. It's a long piece of wood with a crack that runs the length of it, and Hafiz has tried to cover the old name. It used to say *GAZA ZOO*, carved into the wood in block letters. Hafiz has painted over the carving in black and done his own sign in bright yellow. It says *HADIQAT AL HAYAWANAT FOR SUNNY DAYS*. The lettering was done by hand, and the paint is flaking off. The carved letters still show through. I don't want to hurt his feelings, so I say nothing, but Hafiz could have done better. He could have tried a little harder.

But there is a breeze bringing the scent of blossoms from the olive tree nearby, and the sun is warming my back. This could be nice.

My new home is a large pen flanked on each side by other enclosures. I share a chain-link partition with each of my neighbors. I have dry grass, a few boulders, and plenty of space to walk around. Hafiz has brought a few of my things—my long rope with knots, my favorite bucket, and one of my tires (I have three)—and stacked them in a corner. He has made a kind of little house, so that I can feel as if I am in my stable. On one side is a row of four large cages. In the one closest to me, he has put the lions. If I trot across my space to the other side, there is another row of smaller cages, and the one next to my pen has a trio of peacocks. Hafiz said that the lions like me, and that being next to me will make them feel less homesick, and that it will be good for me to be with them, whatever that means. I don't know who is supposed to make *me* feel less homesick.

I don't feel like talking to the lions. It's their fault that I'm stuck here. I pick up my bucket and drop it a few times and push around my tire simply to pass the time. When night falls, I wander into my little shed to sleep. But I can't bring myself to lie down, so I doze on my feet, dreaming of nothing.

In the morning, before I open my eyes, I almost convince myself that I'm still at home. But the smells are different. The air smells more open. Earthy. And I can't detect the woody smell of the older boards that made up my stable. And yet. With my eyes closed, I can still imagine myself there. And if I am there, Hafiz will come in to brush me. He will refill my water. Give me oats. Hold out his hand with a treat, since last night I was so good. And everything will feel exactly as it was before. Then I hear a noise that I haven't heard before.

Today is the first full day that I will spend apart from Hafiz.

I emerge from my shed and examine what I suppose I will call the cage to my right. It's big enough, as far as I can tell. Iron bars, a large tub of water. Some scattered boulders. A large wooden box with a square opening in one end. The same hard-packed dirt that covers my space. And the lions. Tangled up in a snoring lion knot. The female sprawled on her back. The male with his chin tucked over the female's neck so they fit together like one beast. As if there is no end and no beginning between these two cats.

"Hey," I say. Nothing happens. I walk right up to the iron bars and mesh separating our spaces. "Hey," I say again, louder. They stir. The female's back legs stretch slowly. Their tails start flipping

11

back and forth, sending flies stirring. The male raises his head and yawns, his mouth transforming into a gaping cave. I retreat a few steps and watch them untangle themselves and roll apart.

The male stands and blinks at me several times.

"Well?" I ask.

"Well, what?"

"What are your names? What should I call you?" I don't want to call out "Hey" every time I have something to say.

"I am Baqar, and that is Baisha." He looks over at the female who has rolled onto her back again and is staring at me with her head twisted upside down.

"Are you mates?"

"We are brother and sister." Baqar turns away from the partition and walks over to Baisha. He licks the top of her head and flops down next to her. "We are a little pride of two."

"You behave like mates," I say. All that closeness. All that being-next-to-each-other. I don't like it. It's rude when I am here in my enclosure all by myself.

"We have been apart," says Baisha. She pushes her head into her brother, rubbing the side of her face on his paw. I look to the side. I'm not sure whether I should look at them or not. I've forgotten what the rules are for lions.

"Where are the others?" asks Baqar.

"What others?" Nobody has ever asked me this before.

"The others like you. Your brothers and sisters. Your parents. Where are they?"

"I don't know," I say. I didn't know I was supposed to have others. I look over at my pile of belongings, which seems pitiful and ridiculous now. "I have Hafiz, and also . . ." I trail off. My whole life I have had only Hafiz. And now also this zoo.

I don't know much about other zoos, but I know Hafiz is proud of this one. It isn't large, but he talked to me the whole time he was putting it together. I know he has peacocks, and two different kinds of monkeys, a porcupine, and a pair of lemurs. And he has a small herd of goats for children to pet. It isn't big, but I think it can be lovely. He used to walk me through the old grounds, pointing out the new cages and enclosures here and there as everything came together. He is proud that we are not too far from the seaside. Even though I don't want to live here, I have to admit it's nice.

"Those men that brought you were strangers," I finally say.

"They were ours," Baqar says. "And they searched for Baisha because they knew we belong together. They found her with thieves in a tiny cage. The tip of her tail had been cut off. The shame." Here he pauses and licks one of her ears several times. Baisha looks up at me from under the canopy of her brother's head. She flips her tail around her feet, and it is then that I notice the scarred end, un-tasseled and somehow more vulnerable than what I imagined.

The shame. I can see it now.

At dusk on the second night, I hear Hafiz's voice murmuring to the lions. I walk to the other side of my enclosure and linger near a fence post. Hafiz isn't looking at me, but he could see me if only he would turn his head. I'm close enough to hear his voice as he pushes two metal bowls through a low, hinged metal door in the back gate of their enclosure. "I'm sorry," I hear him say. "This is all I have today." He stays to watch them eat, and I can hear the bowls scraping the surface of the earth as the lions devour whatever is in them.

Night falls like a curtain, snuffing out the last light of dusk. Sometimes I can see that things are beautiful here, but when night comes it feels like a shroud. I want to see what Hafiz will do when they are finished eating, so I stay where I am. But all he does is quietly reach back through the door to take the bowls away. When he walks away after shutting the door, he comes inside my enclosure. At first he says nothing. He just reaches out and runs his hand down my nose, pets my ears. I can smell the sea on him, and I know that he went fishing today. And then a memory overtakes me without warning of a day when Hafiz took me to see the ocean. We walked through the market, and I carried his things. *It's beautiful here*, he said that day. *What does this beauty mean if I can never leave it, if I can never long for it?* I kept looking toward the sea. And all I could see was deep blue extending forever.

"Habibi, I know you're angry with me," Hafiz says now.

"You left me behind," I say.

"I know—I'm sorry. But I had to."

"I don't like being left behind, Hafiz. I don't like being away from home."

"It's just for a little while, habibi. Maybe we won't always have checkpoints, and maybe someday I can cross the border to bring over a real zebra. And then I can bring you home." He reaches out and runs his hand down my nose again. "Look: I brought you something." He slides his other hand right under my lips, his palm open flat. Carrots! He stands with me as I crunch through them. And then he kisses my forehead and walks away. I want to watch him quietly. I want to let him have the evening, but Baqar's question tugs at me.

"Hafiz, wait," I call. He pauses and passes his hand over his hair. I watch the breeze gently ripple the fabric of his shirt. I think that he will continue walking, will let the darkness swallow him. But he turns and walks back to me. He stares at me and says nothing. His eyes are the only question. "Hafiz, do I have parents?"

"Do you have parents?" A smile is beginning to spread across his face, and I am afraid that he will laugh at me.

"Yes, Hafiz. Parents. I want to know if I have them."

He steps closer to me and places one palm on my forehead and one on the side of my face. In that moment I remember him placing his hands on me this way long ago. I was smaller. The world was bigger. The olive trees were in bloom. The memory is so tattered that I can grasp little else about it. Only his hands.

"Everybody has parents, habibi," he says, bringing his face closer to mine. "It's how we are born. I have parents. You have parents. We all have parents."

"But where are mine?" I search his face. I want him to tell me that they are waiting for me somewhere.

"Habibi," he says and lets his hands fall from my face. He steps back and looks away into the dark of the night. "I think about them all the time. They belonged to my friend Jaleel." I keep watching him and listening. We have never visited with Jaleel. None of his friends are named Jaleel. "We were children together. He lived in Jabalia Camp, and his family had two donkeys that would carry things for him to the souq." Hafiz does not look at me as he tells this story. "Building a zoo was something he wanted to do, actually. He loved animals. There was this toy he had when we were small. It was this little model of a lion. And it had a mane that he swore was real fur, but I don't know. He wouldn't let me touch it. I teased him every time I saw him. Jaleel and his lion."

"I don't know him," I said. "Where is he?"

"He's gone, habibi." I wait for Hafiz to find his words. I'm afraid to know what it means for him to be gone. "It wasn't a war, really," he says after a while. "At the time, everyone said it was just an escalation. A drone. Someone at a base right over the border sitting at a computer station who saw him on a screen; some pixels that made up Jaleel on his way from the souq, and . . ." Hafiz is silent for a while, his hand over his mouth. He looks up at me finally, tears brimming his eyes. "Jaleel, you know, and his two donkeys, they didn't . . ." he trails off. "It could have easily been me. Tomorrow it could be me. Or next week."

Have I said that Hafiz doesn't sleep most nights?

He rubs his face as if to clean it of his memories.

"It was right after you were born. I told his parents that I would keep you for only a few days, habibi. To help them. He was their only child. His father always said he would come retrieve you. But a few days turned into a few weeks. Which became a few months. And you became mine. And the truth is, habibi, I couldn't let you go. You were so stubborn; mostly legs and your serious face. But your parents, when I think of them, I like to imagine they are in Jannah now."

I can't hear Hafiz anymore. Instead I feel as though I am living outside my own body. I look over and see myself, a lonely

16

donkey standing before a lonely man. I don't know what to say. I want to wail, but I don't, because no sound I can make will match what I feel. I try to remember my parents. I think that I should. They were mine; I need to remember them. But all I can see in my mind are images of my own long face looming over me. I will keep trying to do this for days afterward. That I can't will be a thing that torments me.

"What about yours, Hafiz?" I ask. "What about your parents?"

"They are in the West Bank, habibi. I can't see them anymore. I can't get through." He reaches into his pocket and retrieves a rectangle of folded paper, which he carefully opens. The paper is fragile at the creases, as though it has been bent along these lines thousands of times. "This is us," he says, pointing at a spot on the map near the sea. "And this is the West Bank, where my family is." He draws his finger along a wandering handwritten line up to a point farther up the map. "And that is the road I would take to see them if I could."

"When did you last see them?"

"It has been nine years."

"Do you remember their faces?"

"Yes, Alhamdulillah, I do."

By the third day, I realize that since I won't be going home with Hafiz just yet, I'll be lonely if I don't make an effort with my neighbors. I wander over to the partition and stand next to it, watching them. Their eyes are closed, so I stomp my feet a couple of times and make some huffing noises to see if they will wake. Nothing. I trot over to my things and return with my knotted rope. I fling it back and forth a few times, and the end of the rope hits the partition. Baisha's ears twitch once or twice, but neither lion looks at me. I'd forgotten that lions sleep so much. I grab my bucket and drop it on purpose to make some noise, but they keep ignoring me. This will take more, I think.

"So, hello," I say finally. Baqar's eyes open slightly and rest on me. He blinks twice, yawns, and stretches his front paws out before rolling onto his back and looking at me with his head upside down.

"Hello," he says.

"Do you always sleep this much?"

"I need to visit my dreams." He yawns again, and I see Baisha open her eyes and stretch. This isn't easy. I look around. Kick a clod of dirt at my feet.

"Hafiz is my only friend," I finally blurt out. "I need somebody to talk to."

Baqar nods.

"Has it always been the two of you?" Baisha asks. She has wandered over to the partition that separates us and licked the metal before settling next to Baqar.

"Yes."

"And why exactly did he paint you like a zebra?" She is so curious.

"For the children."

"Yes, so you've said. But why not get a real one?"

"The tunnels are closed now. Hafiz can't get one through." The lions stare at me wordlessly. "Smuggling," I say. "From Egypt. It's how Hafiz got most of them here." I toss my head in the general direction of the zoo at large. They are silent. And I don't know if it means I should go on. I'm not sure how to explain how it feels to us to live in this city. The way that it seems as if a hand reached down and gripped all of us, squeezing until we couldn't move. Hafiz would sit late at night in my shed, hay dust hovering around his head as he ran through lists of animals that he wanted but could not find. I want to tell them about the map I saw the other night. How Hafiz folded it carefully again and slipped it in his pocket. How he carries that road with him. What it means to me that I didn't know. But my tongue feels too large in my mouth. "It's just something I have to do," I finally say. "I have to be the zebra."

"I think you will make a good zebra." Baisha walks right up to the partition. "Come here," she says, looking right at me.

"Why?"

"Just come here. Come next to me." I walk to the partition and hang my head down near hers. She gets as close as she can and sniffs my face. I feel her breath. Warm. Her dark nose dances around me like a flitting insect. I realize that, from far away, it looks like the silhouette of a cup with a stem. This close, I can see it is damp and glistening. She smells like so many things that are foreign and familiar to me. Earth. The meat she ate earlier. Baqar. And faintly of Hafiz. Of his hands. She stretches her pink tongue out of her mouth and gently flicks the end of my muzzle with it. "I see who you are, then." She steps back two steps and stares at me.

"Yes, that is who I am." And so it is that I have made an animal friend of my own.

It is with the lions that I learn to not be afraid of the children. I like the idea of them, but the first time that I see them in person, they dart up to the fence in swarms. Their hands reach out to me. Their eyes are wet. Their voices call out. *Alhimar alwahshiu! Alhimar alwahshiu!* I am afraid to let them touch me. On the first day, it feels like a thousand hands are reaching toward me. I run to the back of my enclosure and grab my knotted rope. I will throw it at them. And if that doesn't work, I will bite them.

"Stay back!" I yell at the lions. "They are dangerous!"

Baqar is deliberately standing close to the children, rubbing his face against his cage, with hardly any distance between his face and their hands.

"They aren't dangerous," Baisha says, supine in the middle of her cage.

"I think I'm going to bite them!" I've decided to stay at the back of my enclosure, and I'm running back and forth across the width of it. I want their thousand eyes to see I am strong and healthy and not for grabbing by all those hands.

"Don't bite them," says Baqar. "They don't mean you any harm."

Eventually, I return to the front of my enclosure, and when they rush for me again I start braying. Those horrible honking sounds spew from my mouth, and I can't stop them. But I don't bite any of the children. This also happens on the second and third days. But on the fourth day, Baqar finally tells me to hush.

"They love you," he says. "They think you are a wonder."

And then the next day I look at them. Their liquid eyes. Their small hands. I listen to their voices that squeal at everything. The way they flit about the olive grove like a swarm of little bees. Their reaching, reaching, reaching.

They are a wonder.

And then everything falls apart.

It is on a day when Hafiz comes to me in the morning and examines my stripes.

"Some of your stripes are fading, habibi. I need to paint you again."

"All right," I say. Secretly I am pleased. I don't get any time with Hafiz anymore. He walks me back to my old stable, and when I step inside and see the filtered light streaming between the slats of wood, I feel at home. I like that there is a roof. My bed is here. My brush is here. All my things. I inhale deeply. My hay. My oats. The dirt I have pressed hard with my own feet. The smell of Hafiz lingering from the times that he was too tired to go to his own house and slept in the stable with me. Sharply absent is the musky scent of the lions.

Hafiz retrieves his paints from a corner, and we are quiet as he paints a little white here, a little black here. Coaxing the zebra back into my coat. And then a sound comes. A sound like the sky is a stone splitting from the side of a mountain.

The ground shakes, and Hafiz and I run to a corner of the stable. I drop to the ground and squeeze my eyes shut. I feel a weight pressing on my back. I know it is Hafiz when he starts whispering, "Don't move, habibi. If we are still, we will be all right." We stay huddled together as we listen to yelling outside in the streets. The ground trembles once more. After a while, a kind of quiet returns, but it's different from other times. It feels as if the quiet is choking me. Hafiz stands up and walks to where he usually keeps my brush. His hands shake as he reaches for it.

"We can take the stripes off, habibi. You don't have to go back to the zoo. I will go back later to see what's happened there." I stare at him. This is what I wanted. And yet.

"But what about the lions?" I ask. "I need to see them." Hafiz turns to look at me. Runs a hand through his beard.

"If that's what you want, habibi. Yes. We can go together."

We return to the zoo. My paint wasn't dry when the air-strike came, so my stripes are smeared and there is paint on Hafiz's clothing. The pathway that winds in front of my enclosure and the two next to mine are littered with debris. I keep stepping over pieces of metal and broken concrete and clods of dirt everywhere. It is a clear and sun-soaked day, and when I look around trying to understand what happened, I see that the olive tree that grew in the little central plaza right across the path has been felled by the bomb. The branches are tangled with splintered wood. An acrid smell merges with the sweetness of the olive blossoms. I look up to see where it all came from, but all I see are two silhouettes hovering overhead. Static in the air, like enormous dragonflies; like dark, angular birds I've never seen before. I want to hide from them, and I look toward the olive tree hoping it can still offer shelter, but before I run I hear a sound like metal scraping metal. I turn from the tree and see Hafiz struggling to open the door to the lions' enclosure. They both lie still on the dirt. They are close to each other. Bodies pressed to the ground. One of Baisha's feet appears tucked behind her like she was waiting to pounce. They are pierced with pieces of shrapnel. They must have bled to death.

Hafiz has forgotten me, and I am suddenly aware that I am out in the zoo the way visitors are. I look at the lions again. The door at the back of their enclosure is twisted and misshapen, and Hafiz yanks at it. He leans back and pulls with the full weight of his body until it snaps open and he falls down cursing. He sits still for a moment. Dust hovers in the air around him. He brings a hand up to his face, and it reminds me of the times I have seen him wipe sweat away with this same gesture. But he leaves his hand there, covering his eyes. And his body starts to shake.

"Hafiz, you have to go in," I call to him. He looks up at me. His eyes are red. But he nods and crawls through the doorway into the enclosure and goes to the lions. He gently examines their bodies. The dirt below them is darkened with their blood, and he turns them as best as he can to find all the places where they have been wounded. I say nothing. I watch him weep and smooth back Baqar's mane. I knew this would happen when I heard the airstrike. We were all so exposed. But Hafiz is just discovering it. He thought we would be fine. That this place, of all places in the city, would be a shelter.

"What are we to do, habibi? I was supposed to keep them safe here." Hafiz wipes his nose on his forearm and then looks up at me. I have nothing to offer.

I decide to stay at the zoo. I can't seem to bring myself to go back to my other life. Things have changed. I have changed.

For a week the lion enclosure is empty. All that is left of them are a few dark smears of their blood on the dirt. Their empty bowls. The ground vibrates with the heavy tanks that pass by on the road outside the zoo. The sound of them rumbling pierces my ears, and I can see them from the spot in my enclosure where I used to stand to talk to the lions. More strange birds cross the sky. I wish that I wasn't here by myself.

And then suddenly the lions return to me.

I discover this on a bright morning when I wander over to our partition. They are lying splayed on their stomachs, a way I have never seen them before. Their eyes are open and cloudy, and they look rigid and dusty. Hafiz has his back to me and is hovering over them with a brush. He is coaxing whatever shine is left out of their coats and trying to smooth Baqar's mane.

"What are you doing?" I ask. He looks over his shoulder at me. Our eyes meet, but he turns back to the lions.

"I'm trying to make them look nice," he says.

"It won't work." Every time I look at them, I see dirt clinging to their coats and I keep imagining them dying. Because we arrived too late for me to see what happened. Shrapnel flying into Baqar's eyes. Slicing across Baisha's throat. I know it is my fault. I wasn't there with them. I should have warned them. Or I should have died instead.

"It has to work." Hafiz keeps brushing them. "I don't know what else to do." He stands up and turns to me, wiping his eyes. "I'm sorry, habibi. I know you were friends." And then he walks out of their cage without coming into my pen.

I look over at Baisha. "What will I do without you?"

"You have to make new friends." It's her.

"I don't know how."

"At first it feels terrible. Maybe you don't like each other. Then you talk again. And then another time. And then many times after that. And then you are friends without knowing when it happened."

24

"Or I could stay here on this side of my pen and talk to you."

"But I'm dead. We're both dead. We don't have anything for you." She sits unmoving, with clouded eyes, as her coat collects dirt.

And so I do as she asks. Talking and talking. Starting over again and again.

But every new friend I make perishes. A boy and his friends bring buckets of water for us to drink, but it's too late; some eagles die of thirst anyway. Three monkeys starve. A porcupine dies in the same drone strike that kills a visiting family. Red ruffed lemurs, tortoise, all dead. I go to the lions, and they tell me to try again. Hafiz has begun letting the few children that still come walk into the cage to pet Baisha and Baqar.

"Try again," one or the other of them says as tiny hands reach out to touch them. "You should always try again."

But it doesn't matter. Everyone is leaving me behind. The crowds of children have stopped coming. Only a few families wander the grounds every few days. They don't seem interested in me anymore. I am lonely, and all I have are the lions. And I'm not even sure about them anymore. They don't move, and their faces are static. I want them to stop speaking to me.

Let me tell you a thing about tragedy. At first, every one of the missiles is shocking. You don't know if you will survive. If you can lose anyone else without losing yourself. And then it becomes ordinary. The sound is muffled. The news of the dead comes to you as if from a great distance and hovers around you like a swarm of flies.

Until, of course, it comes for you. And then everything changes. Everything changes. Everything, everything changes.

And when it comes for me, I remember it all in reverse. There is a crater right outside my enclosure where the path used to be. A jagged bowl in the dirt. I am on the ground with my front legs tucked under me. There is a hum above me. My ears are ringing, and a kind of pressure squeezes my head. Warm liquid runs slowly from my shoulder down to my foreleg. Hafiz drapes himself over my back, weeping. Saying, "I'm sorry. I'm sorry. I'm sorry," over and over again.

And then Hafiz lifts himself away from me. Runs backward toward the gate where he usually enters my enclosure. The words he is yelling rush back into his mouth and down his throat. Blood travels back up my leg and returns to my body. A sound that once was loud compresses itself into a small point and a flash of light rapidly contracts like a flower closing its petals at night. Thin wisps of smoke condense into a thick cloud, which then collapses into nothing. An object rises up out of the crater and flies away whole, and the earth tumbles back into the crater in perfect arcs.

The moment ends with the solid ground beneath me and a clear sky where nothing has ever happened. Where nothing will ever happen.

Tell me how I can learn to live like this.

Afterward, Hafiz helps me stand and leads me back to my stable. He weeps as we walk slowly back home. He weeps as he wipes away my bloody stripes and bandages my wounds. He weeps as he gathers a pitiful pile of oats that I cannot bear to eat. He weeps as he makes my bed out of hay. He only stops weeping when he sleeps beside me that night.

Hafiz will close the zoo soon. There is nobody left who needs a zebra.

It's just us now. Me, and Hafiz, and the holes in the ground.

WHAT WE FED TO THE MANTICORE

They say that life in the Sundarbans revolves around two things: the tide and the tigers.

We are not the tide.

We are the tigers.

It was not what we ate that troubled the villagers, because we had been eating very little. It was what we fed to the Manticore. He arrived hungry. And he could never be satisfied.

We were gathered in a grove of mangrove trees that I had come to think of as our own. They had been special to me. The villagers called them sundari trees, but I knew them as looking-glass mangroves. Their exposed roots stood perpendicular to the ground, like curved knife-edges, wandering in the shape of little rivers. Secretly, I had begun to name each of them. I named one for my mother, and one for the sky. I imagined that they had their own name for me, but they never told me what it was. These mangroves offered a sanctuary I could hide in. I could curl behind the bend of a root blade and stay there for hours, unnoticed. They used to be within my territory, and I loved winding my way among their pale trunks, alone, scratching the bark and rubbing my face against them.

They were mine until they weren't anymore.

I don't remember when we came together. At first it happened little by little. Brother returned to me. Then Small One. And then all at once, there were five of us. The water had become saltier, and sometimes I couldn't drink it without retching. Some of the plants were wilting. All of us had been struggling to find prey. I had been looking for deer tracks, but everywhere I went, I was the first to press my feet into the smooth silt. And so we gathered, dry-tongued, listless, and hungry. Drawn together for comfort, or something like it.

We lay sprawled on a stretch of damp silt a few yards from the bank of a nearby tributary, leaving impressions of our bodies in the earth, so that a villager walking through might understand that a tiger had lain here, or here. The canopy of the trees filtered the sun and cast a moving pattern of dappled light everywhere I looked. If I narrowed my eyes and tilted my head, I could almost see a small deer or a flying fox. But shadows do nothing for hunger, and we were ravenous.

When he came to us, it was dusk, and he was a stranger.

The air was dense and we had not eaten in thirteen days. We were lying among a peculiar field of roots that reminded me that the trees will thrive even as we are wasting, that the mangroves are resourceful in ways we have never been. Some of the trees send pneumatophores, traveling root branches, to collect air for them. They pierce the mud and reach straight up so the ground is stippled with breathing spears. This was the space where the stranger found us.

"Sister, who is that?" asked Small One.

"I don't know," I said, bringing myself up a little higher. "It looks like a tiger."

"Are you certain?" asked Notched Ear.

"Either it is a tiger or it is food," said Crooked Tail. Her tail had taken on a permanent bend after it had been broken during a fight with one of her litter mates when she was a cub. She licked her paw and then turned her head to lie on it.

Small One squinted, trying to make out the loping form that was growing in our field of vision. "It looks too large to be a tiger. What if it thinks that we are the food?" She moved closer to Crooked Tail and started chuffing, looking for comfort. Some of us still thought of her as a cub.

"Maybe it isn't a tiger," I said. I stood up and took a few steps toward the stranger to get a better look, but feeling exposed, I walked back to the others and tried to settle down.

"We can't take on another one," said Brother. "There is nothing to hunt and there's no room in the grove for anyone else."

"No," I said, looking again. Looking more carefully. "That is not a tiger." Its fur was almost familiar, but not quite. It was a glossy continuum of deep red. No stripes.

I raised my head when the stranger came close and saw a man's face nestled in his mane, also red. The fur was lush, and I had an urge to groom it for him. He looked down on me and smiled, baring three rows of neat, sharp teeth.

"I am here," he said. The others looked at each other and then at me, their eyes saying things like "tiger" and "not tiger," refusing to commit to either one. Then they lowered their heads and flattened their ears before I had a chance to do the same. Small One slunk over to the curve of a nearby root blade. Her belly was low to the ground.

"We haven't been waiting for anyone," I said. I sniffed the air near him. It smelled strange, like plants I did not recognize—and, faintly, like blood. "Perhaps you are looking for somebody else."

"I came looking for you." He had a beautiful voice. Like a bird trumpeting over the forest. It made me feel ashamed of my own.

"For me?"

"For all of you. I am hungry." I was afraid to meet his eyes, so I focused instead on his strange mouth. His gums were clean and pink and glistened with saliva.

"We have nothing for you," I said. "We are hungrier than you are."

"Oh?"

"Yes," I said. The others remained still, using the rest of their energy to keep themselves flat on the earth. Brother was squeezing his eyes shut.

"Nothing to share, then?"

"Nothing." I tried to hold the stranger's gaze but his stare drilled through my own eyes into a corner of my mind. I imagined him slinking in there, looking for something that I wasn't willing to reveal. "We go for days without eating," I finally said. "There are hardly any chital deer in the forest these days."

"Perhaps I should eat all of you," said the stranger. "You're better than nothing."

I swallowed deliberately, understanding that I had made some sort of mistake. I heard quiet chuffing, and at first, I didn't realize that it was me. "Some of us," I said after a moment, and began to regret it even as I spoke, "some of us have gone into the villages."

"And why is that?" he asked. "What would a tiger need with a village?"

"There were cattle. We've eaten one or two of the cows. And when there were no cows, we've eaten the goats, and when there are no goats . . ." I looked down and realized I'd been digging a shallow space into the silt with my paw. I didn't want to say what could have come next. That now there were no goats. That the next step would be eating the villagers, but that we weren't willing to go that far. That we had chosen to go hungry. I knew he would never tolerate staying hungry himself. But he understood my silence, and I hated myself for letting him think that a village without cows or goats was still a thing that could be ravaged. When I glanced at Brother I saw that he had bitten off the top of a pneumatophore.

"I see," the stranger said. "The village." He stood for a while looking at things. I watched him cast his eyes to the riverbank. The water moving swiftly in a nearby tributary. The rustling mangrove leaves. Our grove. Us. Me. And then he turned and walked toward the thick of the forest.

"That is not a tiger," I said, to no one in particular. I felt that we had escaped something by a narrow margin.

"What is it then?" asked Small One. She peered at me over the edge of the root blade.

"That is the Manticore," I said as I watched his haunches sway. And I watched his scorpion-tipped tail start to whip. And I watched him shrink into the distance.

The Manticore told me he was in the mood for hunting. I was lying among the mangrove roots, watching him pace the border of our grove of trees. I had been gazing at the silver scales on the underside of the leaves and picturing the night sky. Earlier that day, I had marked the trunks of the outer trees, but the Manticore had come in anyway.

"Will you come with me?" he asked. He looked over the edge of the root blade where I had burrowed into its curve. From my hiding place, it felt as if he was towering over me. My tree had given me up.

"I'm not hungry." That was a lie. And he knew. He had been watching me for hours and had seen me lapping salt water. Rubbing my cheeks on the root spears. Curling into myself to sleep. Not eating.

"I can feed you."

"I don't want what you've been eating."

The night before, I had come upon him on my way back to the grove from a river crossing. He had a man in his mouth. The man's body was bloated and swollen—he must have drowned before the Manticore found him. His lips were unnaturally huge and his tongue poked out of his mouth. His eyes were open. The Manticore saw me and held my gaze, and then bit down firmly on the man.

Now, as he paced, I tried to avert my eyes. I hoped he didn't have another corpse tucked in the brush behind him.

"I have to go," I said. I stood up and stretched, perhaps a little longer than I needed. I didn't want him to follow me.

"And where are you going?" he asked.

"Nowhere," I said.

"Hunting?"

"No." And then I thought better of it. "Maybe. I thought I saw a chital. Unless you've eaten it already."

"Eaten what?" The Manticore stared at me.

"The deer. Have you eaten it?"

"No."

"Well, I'll hunt it then." I turned to go. I walked toward another crossing on the riverbank. It was deeper water but I wanted some distance between us. The Manticore felt otherwise, and followed me. I felt him staring.

"Would you like to solve a riddle?" he asked.

"No," I said, still walking away.

"Not even one?" He had caught up to me without losing his breath. We walked together, with the Manticore leading the way. He kept whipping his tail back and forth. Its scorpion tip barely missed my face each time.

"I wouldn't know how to solve one."

"If you solve it, I will leave you alone."

"Go away."

"As you like," said the Manticore. He coiled himself low to the ground and sprang forth across the widest part of the river. I saw him land effortlessly on the other side and then disappear into a dense patch of mangroves.

"Watch this," the Manticore said. It was dawn and I hadn't eaten for sixteen days. "I'm going to eat that one." I followed his line of sight from the reeds to the center of the river. A dinghy was slipping along the water. Two men were in the boat, murmuring to each other, as though they were trying not to disturb the morning.

"Which one?" I asked.

"The one in the back." He stared at the man crouched near the stern, pushing a long pole into the river bottom in time with his partner at the prow. I knew him, the man in back with the pole, the man unknowingly tempting the Manticore.

"Don't eat him," I said.

"Why not?" the Manticore asked.

"I know him."

"I don't care." And the Manticore darted down the bank and within seconds had crept into the river. I watched him swim quietly behind the boat, his head barely above the water's surface.

I thought of how I had met the man. How once during an unquiet storm I had been separated from my mangroves and carried into the village by an overflowing tributary. The village was stripped of trees. I didn't know how to be a tiger without the forest. I had been swept into a shed near the man's home. I was soggy and confused and curled up against the wall farthest from the doorway. When he turned on the light and saw me illuminated in the harsh glow of a single naked bulb, he inhaled sharply and wiped rain from his face. I could hear the voices of other men calling to each other. Looking for tigers. Planning to kill the ones who had intruded upon the village after the storm. Hungry tigers. We stared at each other, this man and I. He held a rifle in one hand and it was pointed at a corner of the shed. It wobbled unsteadily. His other hand gripped the worn door frame. His breathing was labored, and I saw a throbbing vein in his neck. The shed smelled like ocean water and mud and waste from the man's livestock. I could smell his sweat through the other odors. I inhaled deeply and grimaced so that I could capture as many scents as possible, but I couldn't smell any other tigers. I felt profoundly alone. We stared at each other and then he quietly backed out of the building. He closed the door partway and called out to the others that there were no tigers in his shed. No tigers on his property.

"Leave him," I said to myself as the Manticore slunk up alongside the dinghy, undetected. The man's honey mask was sitting askew, pushed back on his head. Its plastic, rigid face, with a painted beard, was a poor substitute for his own. He was clean shaven. He was old enough to have a child, but young enough that his face still held the echo of the boy he had once been. I closed my eyes.

"Not him," I pleaded as I watched a gentle breeze ripple the cotton fabric of the man's shirt. As I watched the sunrise glint off the dinghy's metal hull. As I saw the man lean over and skim the surface of the river with his fingers. As I saw the reflection of the sunrise in the river break apart and scatter.

The Manticore flung one wet paw over the edge of the boat and I started pacing along the riverbank. The man turned too late, and the Manticore swiftly struck him with the other paw and dragged him into the river with his teeth.

I started chuffing quietly, comforting no one, when I saw the Manticore drag the man to the opposite bank of the river, leaving a trail of blood in the water. I watched the man's partner, who had been left behind at the prow of the boat, alone and weeping.

Shame when the man's honey mask drifted to my side of the shore. Shame when I picked it up gently in my mouth and took it back to my grove of trees. It smelled faintly of coconut. It tasted like plastic.

I wished the Manticore would leave us.

"Are you ready to hunt with me yet?" The Manticore stood over me. Sun filtered through the leaves of the mangrove canopy, scattering their silhouettes across the ground. I looked up at their silver undersides, but I couldn't imagine the night sky anymore. I hadn't eaten for nineteen days. I didn't know how long I'd been sleeping. I raised my head and looked over my shoulder to see my own form stretched along the sand. I was diminished. I was sinking into the landscape. My fur was fading. Orange dissolved into tawny. Tawny faded into beige. I was almost the color of the sand. Indistinguishable from the silt and roots. Ready to be washed away by the river.

"No," I said, resting my head on my paws again.

"Will you ever be ready?"

"No."

When I think of it now, I realize we couldn't have stopped him. Even if we wanted to. No matter how often he is fed, a Manticore is always unsatisfied.

I was swimming through a river crossing when I felt the air become heavy. I struggled to draw it into my nose. By the time I found the Manticore winding his way among the roots of a strange mangrove, one I did not recognize, the wind was twisting its branches, bending them to the earth.

"What is happening?" I asked.

"You will not eat them," said the Manticore, "but that doesn't mean that they will never be eaten."

I walked alone to find our grove, but the paths had changed and I was afraid I would become lost. The plants were cowering from the strong wind, and the river surged in the wrong places. I tried to cross a tributary at three different points and backed away each time because the current looked too strong for me. I saw strange items traveling swiftly down the rushing waterways. A child's toy. A bowl. A tattered book. I was frightened, and I didn't feel like a tiger anymore, just a feeble attempt at what I believed a tiger to be. I was nearly worthless. I thought I should offer myself to the Manticore. He would eat all that was left of me—then no trace of my emptiness would remain.

When I came to our grove, only two of the others were there.

"We were thinking," said Notched Ear, "that perhaps the Manticore is right. Perhaps we should have eaten the villagers."

"He is wrong," I said.

"We are hungry," said Small One. "He will probably eat all of them. There won't be any left for us."

"I don't want us to become like him," I said.

"It doesn't matter," said Notched Ear. "The village thinks it's been us all along. I found two new traps today. And Small One was almost shot. They are looking for us." He turned away from me and made his way down a sodden path toward the river.

"Where are you going?" I asked.

"I'm going to eat," he said. "I'm going to snatch one of the villagers from a boat, like he did." As he walked away, he leaned into the wind, as though it was determined to push him back to me.

"It's too late," I said to myself. I lay down in the silt and felt its fine wet grains soak into my coat. I ignored Small One when she stole away to the bank of a different crossing. I lay alone among my mangrove roots, watching the sky weep. Watching the wind fell trees that had withstood all the other storms I had ever seen. Listening to the surge of the water as the entire web of the Sundarbans waterways swelled over the embankments that shielded the land. Knowing that this was much bigger than the last storm, bigger than all the storms I had seen since I was a cub. Imagining that the furious sea followed close behind, pushing salt water into the network of land and rivers so that all that would remain when the storm subsided would be the stripped earth, and the birds, and the sea.

The sky was dark and mottled when the Manticore found me. Broken branches enclosed me like a cage, and I was partially submerged in the seawater that had washed in. Little rivulets of muddy water ran from my coat. I saw his feet before I saw the rest of him. They were powerful and inexplicably clean. His red coat was still glossy and beautiful despite the dust and water and muck brought in by the growing storm.

"Are you ready for a riddle now?" he asked.

"No," I said. I was too defeated to think about anything.

"Are you sure, tiger? I'm still hungry, and I'm growing tired of the taste of the villagers."

"You're going to eat me anyway," I said.

"Maybe not. I'll give you a simple one. What flies higher than a kingfisher, swims deeper than a whale, and is master of the land and the tress?"

"I don't know."

"Try to answer." The Manticore looked as if he was smiling at me. Benevolently, almost, and with pity. I said nothing. "It's a cyclone, tiger," he went on. "You should know that." The storm was making it difficult for me to see. The rain cut the sky like claws shredding bark. The Manticore seemed as though he was speaking to me from a few steps away and from a great distance all at once. I blinked once or twice and only felt more confused.

"You failed my riddle," he said.

"And you're going to eat me now."

"Yes." He stared at me quietly and neither of us moved. I thought about my mangroves. How I would like to say good-bye to each of them. How I had already forgotten all their names.

"What will be left of me when you're finished?" I asked.

"Nothing," the Manticore said. "I will leave no bones." And he opened his mouth wide, baring three rows of neat sharp teeth.

There are so many stories to tell in this world. There is the sleeping girl, the old man with regrets, the captive princess. There is vengeance on parents; there are star-crossed lovers, adventurous youth, and all different kinds of lonely people. There are heroes, and villains, and quests. And then there are all the stories about the animals and magical creatures.

Or maybe there is only one story. A living thing is born, it moves through the world, and then it dies. For this story, it's less about the telling and more about the retelling.

Maybe, instead, it happened like this.

In the end, there was nothing left of the village, because everything was taken by the Manticore.

Life in the Sundarbans revolves around two things: the tide and the tigers.

He was the tide, and we were the tigers.

We were hungry, but would not eat. He was ravenous and would not stop eating.

First he ate all the deer. And then the monkeys. And then he ate the peacocks, and the fishing cats. He cracked open the shells of turtles and ate the meat inside, and afterward he licked the shells like they were bowls. He peeled back the skin of crocodiles and ate them while their bodies were still twisting and rolling in the water. He snatched flying foxes midair, and bit through all the pangolins, one by one.

When he had eaten all the animals, he turned his hungry jaws on the villagers. He pulled them off boats and out of kitchens. He followed them to forest hives and ate everything but their honey masks. He left no clothes; he left no bones.

And when he tired of eating people, he tried to swallow the village whole. He opened his mouth wider and wider until he became the mist drifting everywhere. Until he became the heaviness of the air that pressed down on the remaining villagers. The Manticore became the sharp wind and the grit and the water that swept in to decimate everything.

And the Manticore became the storm that knocked children down and pushed grandfathers up against crumbling walls. And the Manticore leveled homes. And the Manticore felled trees. And the Manticore tore down power lines and sent them whipping to the earth, like crackling serpents. And he surged over embankments. And he came down on the villages in torrential, unending curtains of rain.

And the Manticore became walls of water rushing in to drown us, drowning us, drowning everyone.

And the Manticore became the sea.

And the Manticore consumed us all.

SOMEONE MUST WATCH OVER THE DEAD

"It is a pity you are so ugly," an eagle said to me once. I wasn't long from fledging but I was grown. "But you vultures are all ugly, doesn't matter what kind," she said. She bent over her talon and worried at it with her raptor's beak, and then stretched her dark wings wide and let the air lift her into a clear sky. I was left behind on an outcropping of rock over a deep valley. I felt a breeze move through the feathers of my neck.

"I am not ugly," I said to the wind that remained, "because I will be of use."

It is said and known by almost everyone that our ancestors fed at the sky funerals in the Place of the Dead. There on the verdant hill, in the middle of that sprawling city, thousands of kilometers away. In the beginning there had been a forest. Light filtered through the closed canopy of the trees and came to rest on the forest floor. Moss and climbing vines wound their way around fallen trees. Creatures made their home among the teakwood. And then the dakhma arrived. Nested among the grove for the canopy to shelter it, but open enough to the sky to invite us in. A city grew up around it. And yet, as the city grew, as the city flourished like a wandering vine, as its tendrils of first stone

49

and then concrete stretched out into the forest, as its roots filled in parts of the sea near the coast, as it rose up toward the sky, the dakhma stood alone. The dakhma stood alone and the dead came, attended in silence.

"Describe it to me," I would ask my father. "I want to see it in my mind."

"What for?" he would ask. "We are not there. It does not need us anymore."

"But we used to be there. It's where we are from. We are rooted there." My father would glance at me. One sideways look for only an instant. And then he would direct his gaze back out at the horizon. I would only ask these questions when we were perched alone.

"We are not trees," he always replied. "We do not have roots. We are only from where we are."

"But what was it for us? What was the dakhma?"

"It was a place where our ancestors were of use." It would go this way, these conversations, every time. But I didn't understand this rootlessness. When I gripped the branches of a tree, I felt that I joined the tree. That we were one living thing that reached from the sky where I perched down into the darkness of the soil where roots reached into places I have never been. I imagined them gripping the earth like talons, holding the tree there in one place as the world moved around it. Why didn't we have roots? What is there to drifting the way we do?

"Tell me about the dakhma," I would always say again.

"The people that came to the teakwood forest made nested rings of stone walls," he would say. "Three or four of them, one inside the other getting smaller. They built them on a hill in the forest." He never looked at me when he told this story. "They would place their dead on the tops of the wall and then they would wait for our ancestors to come and feed."

"Because we were meant to? Because it was our duty?"

"Because the dakhma was of use to us, and we were of use to them. That is all."

My father is dead now. My mother is also dead. I cannot ask about the dakhma anymore.

It is known and it is also said by almost everyone that our ancestors taught all their descendants that it was their duty, the duty of all vultures, to pick the dead clean of their flesh. To speed their transition. To accept their last gift. And so these great birds would dive from the sky, shaping the air under their wings to lift them or send them plunging to the circles of the dakhma.

It is also known and said by almost everyone that many of our ancestors died in that sprawling city with the dakhma on the hill. The forest was shrinking. And a sickness came. The carrion in the city carried a poison. After feeding, our ancestors felt themselves turning to stone and they were no longer able to swoop down on the rings from above. Their feathered bodies were left to rot alone. So it is thought that their transition was delayed and their souls lingered, whispering lessons to the few that remained. One or two of our remaining ancestors, or perhaps two or three, flew north until they came to rest here, where we are now. It is said, even if it is not known, that the open skies called them. Or something else.

These migrants, these nomads, these journeying birds taught the same duties to their young, who taught their young.

And so on. Until it was our turn and we didn't need to be taught. We simply knew, as it was something that lived in our marrow. This service that belonged to us. To come for the dead.

It is said and also it is known by almost everyone that there are some among us that can taste the life that was lived the closer they get to the bone. Not all of us can do this but most of our ancestors, the ones that whisper from the empty dakhma, could. The only vulture among the living who can taste life this way now is called the Lonely One, and it is a thing that she does not necessarily want to do but that she must do, such is her purpose.

It was she who took us to the saiga antelope on the steppe.

We were dispersed and searching for food when the Lonely One called us. A whisper spread from pair to pair and the whisper began with her. *Fly over to the steppe*, it said. So I lifted myself from the low fork of a tree and sailed over the grasses of the dala, the sky spread open at my back, the clouds lofted and rolling, the whisper calling me. It was carrion, we all knew. It was always carrion when we were summoned. Something more than what she and one or two vultures could eat by themselves, perhaps.

At the time I thought nothing of flight, of the way it carried me. It existed almost as a shadow bird that I would rest upon when I took to the air. I paid little attention to the shape of wind at the end of my wings, coursing between the guide feathers. But on that day I felt as though threads were pulling me. Strips of cloth at the ends of my feathers drawing me forward. Air that was no longer malleable, so strong, so persuasive, was the whisper. Had I not wanted to go, I would have gone anyway.

The rocky ledges where we all nested were cast into the distance. I flew to the place where mountains gave way to the even surface of the steppe. The surface of the plain undulating in waves below me like a land-borne sea.

At first it was the most beautiful place I had ever seen. It was enveloped by a wide and endless firmament. I saw that I could soar over everything, following the wriggling curve of the river until reaching the lake that from above was shaped like the eagle's talon. And then I could wheel around again soaring back over the plain. The earth beneath me was even and low, carpeted with wild grass. A place like this was of use to a vulture like me. Carrion was revealed to the sky so easily here. And yet, the beauty and exposure were a trick. There were far too many saiga who had died.

I saw the Lonely One first. Others had already arrived and were gathered in twos, and fours, and sixes at the carcasses. So many of them that it shocked me. It shocked me not that there were so many vultures together at one time but that there were dead so great in number that we might not be able to feed on all of them. That there would be those left without safe passage to what comes next. That there were remains scattered farther than I wanted to see them. Thousands. Hundreds of thousands. Perhaps all the saiga in the world. And the Lonely One. Perched high on an enormous stone. Eating nothing but watching us all.

I flew to the stone and perched beside her.

"Are you not eating?" I asked.

"Not yet," the Lonely One said.

"Will you eat?"

"Yes, but not yet."
"When?"
"When I am ready to know."

The saiga were antelope that used to wander the steppe. I had seen them once or twice before. Before, the sun would move across the sky, rendering their short coats in shades of cream that darkened into gold by dusk. The twists of their delicate horns cast narrow shadows on their faces, which I knew for their wide noses, almost like trunks. They are an old animal. Old like us, watching the earth transform as they live unchanged. They are creatures that belong only to this land. And now all of them have fallen.

"You must eat them," the Lonely One told me. "We must all eat them. It is our duty. It is their gift."

"It is our burden," I said. "There are too many." I didn't know why there were so many.

She looked away from me, and surveyed the sky that enveloped the plains. It was a canopy that held us all in. I thought that I had never seen a blue so vivid as that day. And I wondered if she thought the same.

"It is our duty," she said again.

And so I raised my head to test the wind. I felt the warmth of a current reach out to me. The swell of it buoyed me. I spread my wings wide and let the updraft embrace me.

I landed at the edge of what we began to call the Field of the Dead. A gentle wind ran through the down at my neck, over the bare skin of my head. I closed my eyes to see whether the current wanted to take me away from this field. When I opened them again I saw a calf, curled into the shape of a crescent moon, its nose pressed into the hinge of its folded legs. Dark eyes open to the day, but seeing nothing. A short distance away, the length of my wings outstretched, lay its mother. Her legs were unfolded and she lay on her side just as she must have stood on the steppe before all of this happened. Her neck curved upward as though she had been looking toward the sky and then had fallen to the earth and stayed that way. In her profile I saw the curve of her broad nose, the soft fur of her coat. Her eyes were closed, unlike her calf's. And the light illuminated the short fur of her ears with a delicate radiance.

I went to her first. I thought that if I brought her to the afterlife now, her calf could find her waiting. If that was a comfort of some kind I would give it.

When I pulled away her skin, I saw nothing but the sun glinting off the exposed flesh underneath. I focused then on drawing it cleanly off her body. On the cloudy membrane that was revealed around her muscle. As though she were emerging from an egg. That my consumption of her body was for her, perhaps, a moment of birth again. I thought of the ritual of this. Of what it always meant for me to do this. But when the hook of my beak pierced the meat of her shoulder, I saw the steppe transform before my open eyes. The open sky became streaked with the wisps of thinly spread clouds, luminous at their edges, where they met the blue expanse.

I felt consumed by a dream, submerged in a distorted world as I pulled away strips of flesh and ate them and watched the saiga returned to an earlier time. No longer scattered along the expanse of grassland, they rose like ghosts. A translucent herd, thousands of them gathered as they once did with their calves. I saw this mother, upon whom I fed, bend her aquiline profile to her calf and nuzzle his face, as he stood unsteady on reedy legs.

As I plunged my face into the cavity of her body, feeling the slow seep of her blood dress the skin of my neck, I saw the herd become restless. I felt the heat, the untimely heat, consume the steppe. I felt the saiga fight to give air passage in their lungs.

And it was this way that I learned of the sickness that came. It was the mother's bones that told me.

It had been just one at first. Not this mother, but another one like her. She stood on the steppe and this mother drew in the sweet scent of the wild grass as she watched the other begin to shake her head as though something disturbed her. And then more wildly. She threw back her head, pointing her snout to a blue sky and then violently back again. Trying to dislodge something. To fight something. This mother walked closer, tentatively. And then the other turned her dark eyes on this mother, and the rasp of her labored breathing reached this mother's ears and echoed like the sounds of drowning. Her trunk no longer able to call for help. She was submerged in an invisible, suffocating sea. It was a wretched thing that invaded her body. Or it was a wretched thing that was waiting inside her body. It was, above all else, a wretched thing. And then she fell.

In the beginning of the sickness, this mother and the rest of them, even the fathers and the calves, kept a wide berth from the first lifeless mother. They did not mourn her or inspect her body. They left a ring of empty grass around her. It was still and the air had begun to lie heavy and warm over the steppe.

The herd worried that the same gasping and suffocation would come for them if they ventured too close. They feared that if they grieved for her in the same way they had before, the fever would take root and spread like a vine, ensnaring them all.

But in the days that followed, the air grew heavier and pressed down on them, damp and oppressive. They struggled to breathe. And then they all succumbed, throwing their heads back, seeking the sweet scent of the grass again. When this mother collapsed, it was her own blood that she tasted. Her own body that rose up in her throat to throttle her.

When I lifted my head from the mother's body, I felt as though I had plunged from the sky mid-flight and broken my own frame on the jagged stone edge of a cliff. My bones felt brittle inside me. As though I would shatter if I moved. I had never tasted the story before. I stood in the sun, the mother's blood on my skin, my feathers wet with it. I looked down at her stripped bones as the vision faded and the steppe was silent again.

I did not want to eat this way ever again, but a hunger had settled on me and would not let me go. It was at this instant that I understood who I had become. I turned then to her calf. His body was cool and the cream fur of his face was tipped with lavender. When I pulled his skin away with my beak the images came.

Mother.

Sky.

Grass.

Eat.

The feeling of the earth under hooves.

Breeze moving eyelashes.

The golden sun.

Heat.

Fading light.

There was nothing after that. The briefest life.

It was here that my spirit left me in a rush of cold air. My spirit is the flight that lives in my body. It is the restless thing that lifts me. I stretched my wings wide, spreading the feathers, waiting for the current to reach out for me. But nothing came.

Perhaps this was what was meant for me here: to be tethered to the earth. Because what were these heavy wings for now but to drag along the ground as I walked among the saiga?

I walked, slowly and with my head jutting forward, until I found the Lonely One. She stood on a boulder that was tipped at an angle in the wild grass. A saiga carcass, open and stripped bare, lay before her. The air played through the down and feathers at her neck. Her eyes were heavy lidded as I approached, but they snapped open and she turned to look at me when I stopped near the carcass.

"You have eaten," she said.

"I have. And you have eaten," I replied.

"I have." The Lonely One looked at an empty space beside her on the boulder. And I stepped up to fill the space.

"Is this how it will always be now?" I asked.

"Yes," she said. "This is how it will always be, for us."

It is known and said by almost everyone that time is an immeasurable distance. I understood this as I looked about this plain and saw the horizon reaching out in all directions around us. I felt as though we had always been among the saiga, every generation of us. The world was a dakhma that was too big to understand, and we were at the center. And it was our duty to remain here, watching over the dead.

THE DOG STAR IS THE BRIGHTEST STAR IN THE SKY

In the beginning, there was nothing but the bear. And then he growled and from his icy lungs, the whole world unfurled.

"Tell me a story," said the fox, bathed in the light from a low-hanging moon, the surrounding snow lit by a cool silvery glow. The moonlight touched everything. The fox, her fur fair and glittering; the mountains in the distance; the glacier nestled in a valley leading to the wide expanse of ice fields and snow around her; the sea beyond the coast; and the icebergs that rose up from the dark ocean. The fox was nestled in the crook of the bear's neck, who was himself curled on the snow, his back a jagged mound in the incandescent night.

The white bear.

"Tell me a story," she said again, "tell me a story about the beginning."

"I don't remember the beginning," said the white bear. He yawned widely and sat up, blinking. He looked out at the tundra around him. The surface undulated like a world in miniature, mirroring the surrounding mountains. He thought of the edge of the coast, buried in permafrost, stretching to the sea. The white bear lowered himself again and the fox returned to him.

"It doesn't matter if you remember it. You know it. That's what matters."

"Maybe all I see is the end. Maybe the end is so big that it swallows the beginning. Maybe there is no beginning anymore." The white bear was tired.

"Tell it." The fox pulled her head out of the bear's coat and nipped him in the cheek as if to say again, *Tell me.* The bear breathed deeply and felt the ground beneath him shift.

"In the beginning," said the white bear, "there was nothing but the bear."

"You? The bear is you?"

"Not me, not just any bear. The first bear."

"Yes," said the fox, burrowing back into his coat. "Start again."

"In the beginning, there was nothing but the bear. And then he growled and from his icy lungs, the whole world unfurled. First he spit out the stars. White like snow. Shimmering like snow. And they lit up the world he was making. And then came earth. Dark soil that he shaped in his paws. With his claws he scraped out valleys and pushed the earth into mountains."

"These mountains?" asked the fox. She turned toward the peaks that held in the tundra from a distance.

"All the mountains," said the bear. "He built rolling hills and vast spines of sharp peaks. He pushed some so high that they almost reached his stars. With his enormous paws he spread sand into wide and windy deserts. He scattered rocks and boulders. He bored out caves. He molded the world until his paws ached and he could build no more. And when he looked at all of it, the first bear wept at the beauty of what he had made.

His tears filled the seas and pushed their way through the land into rivers, where they finally pooled into lakes. And when the water touched the soil, all the plants began to grow. The bear growled louder and louder, calling forth all the animals from deep inside himself until all the water and all the land in the whole wide world was filled with life. Birds flew out of his mouth; insects buzzed from his ears; every living thing came from the bear. And then he brought forth the very last thing."

"What was the last thing?" The fox's voice was muffled because her snout was buried in the white bear's fur, but he knew what she was asking. She asked the same question every time.

"You know what the last thing is," said the white bear. He thought suddenly of the icebergs he would see on the next day's hunt. How the ice turned blue at its curves. He thought of the floes that he would ride across the water.

"I want to hear you tell it."

"The very last thing brought forth by the very first bear, was a fox."

"Tell why it was a fox."

"Because the first bear needed a guide through the new world he made. He needed someone to see it with. Someone nimble, who would watch out for him."

"He needed a friend," the fox leapt out from the bear's neck, spun in a circle and curled up once more.

"He needed a friend." The white bear tucked his head around the warmth of the fox's body and closed his eyes against the night. And he dreamed, as he always did, of the world as it was now, the world as it was before he was born, and in the moments right before waking, he dreamed of the first bear.

65

The white bear knew he had been alone for a long time. Ever since he left his mother, he had been alone.

It hadn't always been that way. The white bear remembered being nestled in a snowy den with his mother and his twin. They wrapped their legs around each other as their mother told them stories about how the white bears used to live. All of them together, gathered in crowds on the floes. Riding them like ships. They would travel around the whole world on the ice. An army of white bears. Exploring everything that was theirs; all that had been made by the first bear, who was the mother and father of all the bears.

"When?" his twin had asked. "When you were a cub?"

"No," said their mother.

"When your mother was a cub?"

"No."

"Then when?"

"A long time ago," she said. "Before I was born, and before my mother was born, and her mother."

"Then how do you know how it was? How do you know there were others?"

"I just know," she said.

The white bear and his twin couldn't imagine a home other than their den, and the luminous blue of the packed snow inside. They could not understand a world other than the curves and turns of the surfaces of the glaciers they traveled with their mother. They mimicked her and raised their noses to the air when she began tracking a seal before a hunt. The white bear was astonished at the oily scent of its breath driving over the ice, and he lay on his belly with his twin at the seal's breathing hole that their mother led them to. But when the seal emerged, it was their mother who caught it. She taught them what to eat and what to leave behind.

"For the foxes," she said, "in case they come."

"Like the first bear!" cried the twin.

"Like the first bear," said their mother.

And when the hunt and the feeding were over, the white bear and his twin, drowsy and intoxicated by seal fat, would climb onto her back and cling to her fur as she made her way across the snow to their den. And so it seemed that the three of them were the only bears in the world.

When they were grown, the white bear, his twin, and their mother parted and disappeared from each other as they crossed the tundra. Starting from a single point and then receding into the white.

And then one day the fox came. The white bear tried to remember when she arrived and began to skitter after him like an uneasy shadow, pouncing on his footprints as he plodded across the snow. But the memory kept drifting away from him and he couldn't catch it. Was it . . . no, perhaps it was . . . and then it would slip from his teeth.

"You should go now," said the fox. She hopped from the snow up onto the white bear's shoulder. He was crouched behind a snowbank on his stomach. A long dawn had given way to a short day and they had found a seal. The fox was worried that the white bear would miss it. He had brought them closer to the edge of the coast, following the scent of its breath, but he was moving slowly. When the white bear paused to raise his nose to a stream of air, the fox wound her way around his legs; dancing and pouncing until the white bear moved again. When they finally spotted the seal, the white bear pressed himself to the ground behind a low mound of snow. He lay as still as he could and imagined himself transforming into a hill in the ice fields.

"No, it's too early and you're making too much noise," said the bear.

"But you'll miss it!" The fox jumped down and then up again, sending a spray of glittering powder to scatter in the sun. The deep blue of the sky stretched to the edge of the white bear's vision.

"I don't know where it's going to go," said the white bear. "I'm just watching it."

"A watcher like you will always be hungry. Should I get it for you?" The fox was anxious. The first time she ever saw the white bear was from a distance. She had been crouched over her diminished cache of eggs, and as she sucked the yolk from the last one, she decided she might follow the bear and live on the carcasses he would leave behind. *The bear is alone*, she thought to herself, *like the first bear.*

But now it was the white bear who was diminished. It had been nearly one full ice season and he had caught almost nothing. The fox would pull fish from the edge of the water, or voles she heard under the snow, and share them with the white bear. But these things couldn't hold back his hunger.

"You're too small." The white bear stayed motionless and watched the seal turn its face toward the sun and stretch itself on a vast ice floe. The white bear wasn't sure how close it was, the ice; and also, whether it would hold him. "I'm going now," the white bear finally said. He reached one paw forward and then stalked slowly along the snow, keeping his body close to the ground until he felt the pressure beneath his feet that told him it was now ice that bore him. The seal grew as the bear advanced. Like a dark sun. Like a magnet drawing in the hungry. How many days had it been since the white bear had last eaten?

The fox followed him along the ice, and the white bear imagined her face behind him. The face that by now he knew so well. Eyes and nose dark like the deep sea. Coat white like the snow. She was exactly like the white bear.

And also, she was nothing like him.

They were close enough now that the white bear could see the seal's size, and the gulf of water that had carved its way between the floe and the coastal ice. And the white bear became weary. He thought of this distance as a thing that had no meaning anymore. A thing that stretched and stretched until something broke. And then the broken pieces would stretch again, until they broke again, until the whole world was spread thin and shattered.

The white bear thought that perhaps he would always be hungry.

"I have to go in," said the white bear.

"The water?" asked the fox. "You're not strong enough anymore." She stood near the bear's shoulder and looked out over the gulf between them and the floe, now an expanse larger than the last one the bear had faced. The fox's paws barely made a mark in the layer of snow that covered the ice. She remembered the last time that they hunted together, and failed together. The icy claws of the winter ocean piercing her coat and reaching all the way to her skin. Even after shaking the water from her fur, the chill stayed with her, and at night she had nestled at the white bear's throat, shivering.

In the distance an iceberg, newly calved from the glacier, rose from the water like a desolate island. The white bear saw that the deep blue of its contours was the same as the color of the sky.

The white bear thought of the fox's prints in the snow that same way that he thought about stars. When he watched the night sky, he felt that they rotated around a point and that he sat at the center. And he was at the center of the fox's dancing paw prints as they made their way across the snow, across the ice, and into the sea, where her prints vanished as if into a darkened dawn.

Did she know how much he needed her now? How he didn't remember solitude anymore and would go anywhere she led him, because she was the brightest star?

The white bear leapt over the edge and plunged into the water. He did not wonder if the fox had joined him.

In the grip of the sea, the white bear pressed his ears down, shut his nostrils, and became weightless. When he was a cub, he had been afraid of the ocean. It seemed cold and unforgiving and woven through with currents that would pull him away from his mother and his twin. But now he relished this feeling of being suspended above the inky depths. If he listened carefully, he could hear the whales slipping through the deep as they traveled the whole of the sea. He wondered sometimes what other creatures the first bear had scattered in the water when he made the whole world, and what of the first bear's creation had already disappeared forever.

The white bear began to swim.

He pulled his paws through the water and felt it ripple as it passed between his toes. And he remembered when he and his twin were taught to swim by their mother.

"You will live alone," said their mother.

"But why?" asked the white bear, then just a cub.

"Because there isn't enough anymore," she said.

"Of what?"

"Of anything. There isn't enough ice. There isn't enough food. There aren't enough bears." She stood with them at the edge of the ice as the three of them peered into the sea. "You must learn how to hunt. And you will do this alone. Until you mate and your mate has cubs and they are sent to do this alone."

The white bear and his twin looked at each other and then their mother. They thought separately of their den, and the press of her coat, and how it was she who caught them if they stumbled down a snowbank. The white bear thought also of her milk and how it was warm and it fed him and his twin and how with it there was no need to go into the liquid obsidian of the sea.

"I want to be with you always," the white bear said then, "so I will never be alone."

"It will be all right," said their mother. "You will be like the first bear. The first bear was alone."

"The first bear had the fox. He wasn't alone," said the twin.

"I don't know if there are any foxes anymore," said their mother. "Maybe the foxes are gone." She dove into the water and the white bear and his twin followed her. Buoyed by the air in their coats, they pulled at the water with their paws and stayed close to her. The surface of the ice at the top of the water looked a little like clouds to the white bear and his twin, like a storm brewing above the calm of the sea. Later, as the white bear and his twin stood on the ice and shook the water from their fur, born almost anew after a plunge into the ocean, he looked around at the tundra for signs of a fox. And there was nothing. *I will be alone*, he thought to himself.

Now, as the fox followed the white bear, swimming at the edge of his vision, he remembered his surprise when she arrived. He had been alone, and now she was with him.

He saw the light shift, and he looked for the edge of the ice floe. The fox swam beside him whispering quietly to herself the words of a song the bear could not remember, but felt he knew just the same.

The white bear reached the edge of the floe and saw it had been broken. What had once been a kind of jagged continent had splintered into a diminished icy island.

The white bear surfaced, drew in a deep breath and slipped quietly under the ice, hunting for a shadow, and hunting for the seal.

"It's that way," said the fox. "I can see it." Her voice took on a strange quality underwater. It sounded, to the white bear, as if it was coming from a great distance.

"I know," said the bear.

"It's a fat one."

"Hush," said the bear. He moved further along under the ice, blowing bubbles like pearls. He emerged quiet on the other side. His eyes fixed on the seal's back; smooth and speckled, the sun following the curve of its body; its markings forming a pattern like dark stones scattered across a sandy shore.

The white bear tried to remember the last time he had seen a seal like this. Since the fox arrived, he had seen one, but had failed to catch it. The one before that had been when the white bear was alone. There had been the bounty of a whale carcass once, but that was when the white bear was younger. He had seen other bears at the carcass. Several of them, and they had stood together, close at the shoulder. The white bear marveled at the warmth of them. The steam of their breath. The sounds of their voices. He imagined all of them leaping onto a floe at once and pushing it away from the coast to explore the world together. He looked for his twin, but did not see him among the feeding bears. He wondered if his twin would be familiar to him anymore; they had been apart for so many seasons. When the carcass was spent, they all scattered and the white bear was alone again. The sea ice had come and gone several times now since he last saw any other bears. The ice used to spread further and last longer. But now it seemed as though everything was water and barren land and the white bear would be swimming between them forever.

Sometimes the white bear liked to roll onto his back in the snow and gaze up at the canopy of the night sky or watch the terns flying overhead in daylight. When the fox first arrived,

TALIA LAKSHMI KOLLURI

she would climb onto the mountain of his belly and curl her
nose into her tail. And then she would ask, as she always did,
about the first bear. But as the hungry days stretched further
and further, the mountain of the white bear eroded. Instead,
the fox walked on deft feet across his chest, balancing on his
bones, and curled up at his throat, where the warmth of his
body lingered.

The white bear quietly lifted his head above the surface, tread-
ing water. The fox emerged next to the bear and watched the
seal with him. "Has it seen you?" she asked.

"No," said the bear. "Not yet."

"You should go before it sees you."

"I know." In one swift motion, the white bear rose from the
water onto the edge of the floe, two great paws pushing him
until the whole of his body was on the ice. The floe rocked and
he dove toward the seal. The fox followed. But it was too late.
The seal turned and tumbled into the water.

"Follow it!" The fox cried and leapt into the sea. The white
bear dove in after her. But the seal, ungainly on the ice, trans-
formed into something elegant underwater. It slipped away
from the white bear in curving spirals. And the bear's coat,
saturated by the sea, pulled the speed of his limbs to a crawl.
He remembered a dream he had once of running. He couldn't
remember whether he was running toward or away from
something, but the air in his dream felt like the sea did now.
Thick and cumbersome, reining his legs in so that he couldn't
move fast enough. He was unable to catch anything. Unable to
escape anything. The seal whirled away into the blue, and the

74

white bear was left to return to the floe. He surfaced again with the fox by his side. He lifted one wet paw onto the edge, then another, and then heaved himself onto the surface.

The light above the surface felt as though it would shatter him. So different from the quiet diffusion underwater.

The white bear stood on his hind legs and stretched his body as tall as it would go. He wondered if the first bear had stood like this before he carved out the valleys and wept to fill the sea. The bear's shadow betrayed his hunger. His heavy limbs looked out of place against the concave curves and jutting bones of his torso. Spread out before him was the world the first bear made. Cold, and desolate, and beautiful.

MAY GOD FOREVER BLESS THE RHINO KEEPERS

I am a Hound and I am sitting in the dark, at the very edge of the morning, waiting in the garden for my Joseph to arise so that we can begin to work. I try to remain motionless, so that when he sees me he will know that I'm ready to work, but my ear itches and every so often I give it a few quick scratches. On other days I wait for him in his room, and I sit by his bed staring at him until he opens his eyes. Sometimes I pass the time licking his bedposts. But today I am watching my ash tree in the dark. A breeze is moving the branches and I can hear the leaves touching each other.

When Joseph emerges from the back door of his cottage and into the garden, I see that his slacks and shirt are nicely pressed. His clothes are the color of earth and savannah grasses, which I like very much. His shirt has a name tag sewn onto it. It says, "Wekesa." That is pressed too. The other keepers wear their shirts untucked and their shirttails flap around making noise in the wind, but Joseph always wears his tucked in, which I prefer. It helps me to recognize him from a distance when there are too many smells in the air. I always try to be careful not to get my nose near him once he has pressed his slacks. My nose is wet.

We leave the garden and walk to an armory past the chimpanzee nest that holds my stinking rival, Chiku. Her musky scent overpowers what I know would be the sweet scent of the grassland drifting my way and all I can smell is her foul skin. Chiku is old and is allowed out of her enclosure sometimes. I think she is half-tame but she won't admit it. Once, I caught her building a little stack of stones at the base of a tree in our Conservancy. She muttered at the rocks as she piled them up. I heard later from another hound that she called it praying, which I think might be useless.

I think I hate her.

"Hey, Hound!" Chiku yells as we walk past her, "Hey, you filthy Hound!"

I ignore her.

"I'll be praying for you today." I look back and I see a smirk spread across her face. "I'll be praying for you to get trampled!" She starts cackling and tumbles over on her side into a hammock.

As we walk away, I comfort myself by imagining what it would be like to bite into her fat belly and watch all her guts spill out into the dirt. Nasty chimp.

When we get to the armory, Joseph brushes my head with the tips of his fingers as we cross the threshold. He leaves the lights off and prepares for the day in the dark, cleaning and oiling his rifle, gathering a pack and his GPS tracker. I wander the room sniffing the corners while I wait for him. I smell the dogs that were here yesterday and I try to imagine the day ahead. Look for the rhino. Protect the rhino. It's what we are meant to do.

By the time we are ready to leave, the rest of the keepers have come into the armory with their dogs. Tracking hounds like me, and dogs who have been trained to attack poachers. And today, like every day, before we leave the armory, Joseph leans over me, places his hand on the crown of my head and presses his lips to the spot above my eyes. This gesture has some significance for Joseph, because every time he does it, he closes his eyes. I have lived with him for three years and I still don't know what it means. But I love the feeling of the palm of his hand laid gently on the crown of my head.

We walk past the training boma on the way to find our rhinoceros, Zuri, for our shift. The light is coming and I can see insects gathering in the air, dancing in little swirls above the posts of the boma. Joseph says that Kenya has the most beautiful sunrises in the world, with so many colors. I can't see all of them, but I want Joseph to know that I hear him, so every morning I pause to consider the sky so that Joseph thinks I can see the colors too.

When she arrived at the Conservancy, Zuri spent six weeks in the training boma. And then she gave birth to Zawati, and now they are free to roam the space set aside for endangered species. Two of the last of their kind.

"Come on, Hound," Joseph says, reaching his hand out to me. "Let's go." He glances at his GPS receiver and we set out into the expanse of the Conservancy.

We make our way out into the grassy plains. Before we get deep into the savannah, we pass an old and imposing baobab tree. It has a wide trunk, wide like an elephant, and branches that spread out in a canopy at the top. There is no other tree like a baobab. This one marks the beginning of the wild part of the Conservancy. Past this point, none of the animals that

live there have a Joseph in the way that I do. I love all the
spaces past the baobab tree, but I'm a visitor here. This part
of the Conservancy doesn't really belong to me. Because I am
tame.

When we pass the tree, I start to create a list in my mind
of the smells I come across to make myself useful right away.
I might need to know these smells later. Dirt. Savannah grass.
Dung from another rhino. Dung from a deer. Cheetah scent.
Details emerge in front of me as the morning begins to wash
over our path. Dirt again. The sun is rising and everything
seems lit up from the inside. I think I can almost smell Zuri.
It is a musky, dusty smell. My heart starts to beat faster and I
look around for other signs of her. It's like this every day for
me. Once we venture into the savannah, every second that we
are away from her, every moment that we spend searching for
her, troubles me. I feel pressure and panic mounting. I need to
see her. Where is she?

I hate this feeling.

The dusty smell grows stronger, but now it's also damp. I
realize I've started to hold my breath, but I can't seem to stop.
We turn to walk into the sunrise and I see Zuri's silhouette
ahead of us in profile. I can breathe now. She is still. I can't
see Zawati, but I can smell her nearby. She smells like Zuri,
but with a milky sweetness. When we get closer, I can see that
Zuri has all four feet planted in a pit of sticky mud grunting
with satisfaction. She lowers herself and settles in as we reach
her.

"Morning, old girl," Joseph says as he goes to her. He walks
to her great gray head and, just like with me in the morning,

presses his lips to her forehead and closes his eyes. And like with me, he does this every day. I wonder what it's like for her. I've never asked, but I wonder if she also likes the weight of his hand on her head.

I give them a minute together, but I can't stay away for long. When Joseph opens his eyes, I run up to Zuri. My tail is wagging and I know it's obvious that I love her. I spend a few moments sniffing her to make sure she smells the same as yesterday. She does. When I reach her shoulders, I lick her rough skin. She tastes like the earth and her skin feels like the time I licked a stretch of paved road as a pup. Except supple. And warm. When I reach her face, she hangs her head low and close to me, gently nudging me with her horn. Joseph filed it down a while ago, but it's growing back. I listen to the *huff huff* of her breath as she sniffs my neck, my body. Zuri may be quiet, and she may move slowly, but we are friends. We pause and I look into her dark eyes.

And then I start whispering in her ear, as I do every day. "Tell me where you're going today, Zuri. Tell me so I can watch over you." Sometimes she tells me, but today she just winks at me. "Ah. So is today one of those days when we will play the game?" I lick her cheek. So it is. Today is for the game.

"If you didn't have me, you'd lose all your skills, Hound. I'm playing the game for you." She leans her face toward me and I lick her cheek again. I taste the metal in the dust that settles on her skin.

The game we play is simple. It's called Find Me. I try to find her and she tries to not be found. It was my idea to start playing it. I thought it would be good for her. I thought it might teach her to avoid poachers. I like the game. At least, I will like it as long as she lives.

We sit together for a while. Watching a dragonfly. And then she sighs. Heavy like when Joseph sets a bag down on the floor. "Have you seen Zawati today yet?" she asks. "She's growing so fast." A pause. "And someday she won't need me anymore."

It's been years since a rhino calf was born at the Conservancy. And Zuri's is the first I've ever known.

"Calves just grow and grow," I say, "like they're supposed to. Let me see her." My tail starts wagging and I turn to look for our calf.

I see Zawati peeking out from Zuri's back leg. I want to lick her face, but she doesn't know me quite yet. If I give her some time, she will. She is a baby and is still nursing. She stares at me with her black eyes and then looks away. I try to go toward her but she ducks back behind her mother, hiding her face. I see her tail flicking back and forth. She's not so good at hiding. Today was too soon for me to approach her. I'm greedy. I want everyone to love me.

It took a while for Zuri to warm up to me too. When she first arrived, she would turn around whenever I came near. She didn't want to look at me. I started by licking her legs, right near her feet. And after a while, she let me come closer and closer to her head, until she stopped turning away from me at all. Now on long days, we rest together. If Joseph and I find her in the middle of the day, she lies down and we lean against her. Joseph eats his lunch and I curl up by her flank, feeling the slow draw of her breath. Like a great balloon filling and emptying beside me. Like a slow, long heartbeat. Today, since we found her first thing in the morning, we will leave before Joseph takes his midday meal. But not yet. First Joseph gives her a mud bath. He scoops up great handfuls of mud and smears it on her back in long sweeping strokes, murmuring to her the entire time. He told me once that this is to protect her from the sun and so I wait. By the time he's finished the sun is flooding the grassland with light, and we walk away together to patrol the perimeter.

"Until later, Zuri!" Joseph calls out over his shoulder. He laughs to himself as we walk away, and wipes the mud from his hands with a rag he keeps tucked in his belt.

Now the game of Find Me will begin.

We don't see her again until night has fallen. The moon has started to rise. A thin curved sliver, it casts a weak and silvery light. She stands with her back to us; still as a statue. Staring intently into the forest. She doesn't turn when our footsteps come nearer. She doesn't turn when the sound of my sniffing and lip licking would catch her attention on any other day. Joseph is chatting to me and to himself. When he sees Zuri hasn't turned around, he calls out to her.

"Hey-oh, old girl. Twice in a day! That's new—did you miss us?" She doesn't turn. We walk up behind her and Joseph stops at her hind legs. He places a hand on her flank, pats her gently, and starts to quietly hum a little song that he likes to sing to us. I walk slowly around her in the darkness, and then I hear her whisper to me.

"Don't go any further, Hound. He's here." I don't see anyone else but I grip Joseph's pant leg with my teeth and pull once. A signal to stop. He freezes, his hand still on Zuri. I look up at him and his eyes are wide. His body is tense now and I can feel him snap into alertness.

"Who is here?" I ask her, keeping my voice as low as I can.

"The stranger. I don't like him, Hound. He smells dangerous."

"Where is he?"

"In the bushes over there."

I pause and I take in all the layers drifting through the air, and then I catch it. Something foul and pungent. But also human. I sniff and sniff the air trying to understand what it is. I can think of it only as sort of like an unwashed Joseph. Joseph if he were not neat. Joseph if he had spent his whole life tending a mind full of anger and fear. I learned from another hound once that these kinds of men smell a certain way. You can smell them wanting to lash out and run at the same time. The sourness that clings to a man who is made of a particular kind of raging terror. And I think this is the smell that I catch drifting from a dark patch of brush.

I begin to creep forward toward the smell. Slowly. Quietly. I smell him well before I see him. Him. The poacher. Which is to say I also smell his filthy clothes and his gun, which is not oiled and cared for like Joseph's, but rusty. I smell rust and dirt that doesn't belong here, and also other things.

That I smell him first is neither good nor bad, but soon afterward, I see him. He is a puzzle of shadows in the faint moonlight. And when I see him, I stop creeping forward and move to do the thing that I had been told I may have to one day do, which is to say I rush forward with the purpose of biting him and also of not letting go. Even though I am a tracking hound, and not a fighting dog, I was taught to be ready, just in case. I feel my paws slip at first on fine-grained earth, but I scramble to find my footing on a clump of short grass. I feel my nails dig into the earth and my body propel forward. The mineral scent of silt and gravel rises up around me. My vision narrows to a dim tunnel with a bright point at the center, focused on the poacher. I see his eyes grow wide at the sight of me. I dart at him from an angle, knowing I will reach him with the full force of my body knocking him down.

But he fires his gun. Not well. Not true. But fires it all the same and I feel something searing tear through my foreleg. But I have the purpose of biting him and I have also three remaining legs in good working order, and so though I stumble, I lurch forward again and land my teeth in his flesh. There is hardly any resistance from the fabric of his clothes and after a little push, my teeth drive through into his muscle. But his gun goes off again and also once or twice more. And when I hear a cry from Joseph and braying from Zuri, I realize that I have miscalculated. I know that what I am gripping in my jaw is the man's leg and not his arm or his torso as I should have, because three legs in working order can't propel me as far as four. I know this now.

I turn my head as far as I can without loosening my grip. I can't see much, but out of the corner of my eye, I see Zuri crumpled on the ground. There is a dark mark on her head. I blink once or twice to refocus my eyes and I see it is a hole. The entry of a violent pathway that leads to her brain. And everything that is Zuri runs out, down her forehead in a river of blood.

She is gone.

I think I see Joseph with his body draped over Zawati like a blanket, moving with her. Zawati is crawling to her mother, sniffing her face.

I am still gripping the leg.

The rage then, the rage that I had smelled on the poacher—it becomes mine. I take it from him as I shake my head back and forth ripping the flesh of his leg away from the bone. I see his mouth open wide, his gaping mouth like a cave overtaking his face, his chest heaving, his hand trembling as it reaches for the shredded remains of his calf.

I look directly at the poacher. And I think of my Zuri. My breathing mountain. When I lunge at him one last time, he barely resists me. One arm halfheartedly lifted to his face. His windpipe gives way when I press my jaw closed around his throat. I don't remember anything after that.

"They've taken your leg, Hound." I wake to the sound of Chiku's voice, and find myself on a steel exam room table in the vet building. My head rests in her lap and she is slowly stroking my ears. I feel as if my whole body is a wound. I stretch my front paws and see only one lonely foot reach out in front of me. The place where my leg should be is throbbing. I let the horror sink in, while I realize what it means. It is gone forever. I think about looking for it, or asking for it to be given back. But I'm weary. All the while, Chiku strokes my ears. There I am, damaged and bloody. On the cusp of a life that I will now spend teetering around with not enough legs, being haunted by the ghost of my paw. The one I had favored and used to reach out to Joseph when I wanted his attention, to turn over the sticks that I tossed around in the yard. I am vulnerable in a way that I never wanted to be, wrapped in the stinky embrace of my rival. And yet, I make no moves to leave her.

Chiku comes to see me every day that I am in the vet building. She walks in on two legs. Smacking corners as she turns past them and relaxing her lips into something like a smile when she sees the veterinarian and his staff. She thinks they like it when she shows her teeth. At first she says very little. Just sits and wordlessly runs her hands over my ears. But after a few days together, we both begin to relax. I become used to her. When I smell her coming down the hall toward me, my tail starts thumping and I don't even think to stop it. I use one paw to push myself up so that I can greet her. The scent I once thought was rancid is now somehow comforting. We start to tell each other stories.

"Chiku," I say, "do you remember your mother?"

"Yes," she says. "She was fat and I hated her." We are quiet together. "Also I loved her."

I wonder what I remember of my own mother. Smells mostly. And the velvet feeling of her ear as I slept with it draped over me once. *Oh, Mama!* I feel a black rope of sadness start to twist inside me. *I'm so sorry, Mama! I haven't thought of you nearly enough!* I start to whine and Chiku wraps her arms tighter around me.

After a week has gone by, I'm able to walk on three legs. Chiku was there every day as the veterinarian wrapped a cloth sling around me and held me up until I was used to my legs. And she didn't mock me even once. I don't feel graceful, but now I'm walking by myself. I want to be with Joseph. I want to sleep on my blanket. Walking hurts. No, that isn't quite it. I hurt, and walking feels strange. Something is wrong and I'm trying to figure it out. I feel lopsided and sorry for myself. I move toward the front door, still not quite accustomed to the timing of my steps. I'm going to look for Joseph.

"She won't sleep alone," Chiku calls after me.

"Who?"

"Zawati. She won't sleep alone." It's the first time Chiku has mentioned Zawati since I asked three days ago. "She cries and cries. That was how she was when they found her."

"They found Zawati crying?" I hold myself still in the doorway. I don't turn. The effort feels like it would be too much. So I wait.

"Yes," says Chiku. "They found her crying. Over her mother. Crying while her mother died. Joseph was with her. Wrapped over her body like a shell. He was bleeding too, Hound."

"What happened to the man?" It is the question I do not want to ask.

"What man?"

"The poacher."

"I don't know."

"Why did it have to be Zuri?" The other question I do not want to ask.

"Because she was the one that was there. People are strange, Hound," she says, "they do desperate things."

"Terrible things."

"Sometimes yes. And sometimes no."

"What do you mean?"

90

"There's Joseph."

"What about Joseph?" Joseph who has forgotten about me.

Chiku is quiet and I finally turn to look at her. I see her sitting on the steel table. She is gripping her feet with her hands and rocking back and forth a little bit. I say nothing. Waiting.

"Joseph goes to her."

"He does?" Joseph. I want to see Joseph.

"He's gone every night," says Chiku. "He's stayed with her in the boma every night so far."

I wander back to our garden, alone. I don't wait for Joseph to come get me. If he's spending all his time with Zawati, then he's forgotten about me. When I pass the boma, I look over and imagine Joseph curled up next to Zawati, or covering her like a blanket. I wonder if his bed would be empty if I went to watch him in the morning.

I go to all my corners in the garden. I check for the scent of the other dogs. I pass by one or two of the other keepers, but none of them are Joseph. None of them bend down to press their lips against my forehead. None of them call me to watch them iron their clothing. I'm drifting in the wind, and with no purchase on anything, I may fly away forever.

There's nothing left to do but go to the boma. It's dark when I wander in. I can't smell Joseph, but I look around for him just in case. I find Zawati and crawl into her pen. She's lying in the farthest corner, legs tucked underneath her body. She doesn't move at all, as far as I can tell, and she eyes me timidly. I limp over to her with my head hung low, tail straight out. If I were able to crawl to her on my belly, I would. But I can't. It feels as if it's taking me forever to get to her. It feels like years. When I reach her, I spend a few minutes gently sniffing her face and neck. Her little rhino body. She smells like straw and the formula that the vets are feeding her. I sit next to her, plopping my haunches down close to her chest. Then I gingerly lower the rest of myself, which is difficult and strange, doing it with one leg, until my body rests against hers and my head nestles in the crook of her neck. Her hide is dusty and warm. I feel her settle against me and our breathing starts to harmonize. I think about what it is for Zawati to be motherless. To be haunted by the vision of her mother falling. To feel so alone. I don't begrudge her Joseph when I think of that. I've always had him. I will always have him. But Zawati is navigating her way through a strange forest now.

I close my eyes and sigh. I almost don't notice when Zawati starts to make the quietest sounds. But then her voice elevates to a wail that can't be ignored. It is high and whining, almost like a pup. Or something like the sound I imagine a whale would make when calling to friends across miles of ocean. She is crying. I don't want her to cry alone, and so I start whining with her. And then I'm no longer imitating her sadness. I feel it as my own. I lift my chin and howl, long and ranging, a song of my own anguish alongside hers.

In the morning I wake and find myself still curled up in the boma with Zawati. Sunlight streams through the gaps in the wooden slats that make up the walls of the pen. My bandage is bloody again. I can smell it. Zawati is snoring softly and I try as best as I can to get up slowly so that I won't wake her. I'm struggling to raise myself when I hear a sound and I give up. A sort of rhythmic rustling. Footsteps on straw. It's Joseph. Chiku has brought him here and he stands with her in the doorway, holding her hand and leaning hard on his cane.

He says nothing.

Joseph reaches his hand out to me. It's our signal. The one he uses when he wants me to come to him. But I don't go. My body is hurting again and Zawati is warm. And suddenly I don't want to go anywhere, even though it's morning and it's time for the day to begin. I look down at my front paw instead. At how it looks small next to Zawati's fat and stumpy legs. I look at the straw scattered over the floor. At the dust that drifts down in the sunbeams that are streaming through the gaps in the wood. I look at things that are not Joseph.

He doesn't say anything, but he walks over to me slowly. I can feel him coming closer. I can hear his shoes scuffing through the dirt as he tries to be quiet. I see the tip of his cane. I hear his uneven steps. I know he has a limp now, same as I do. When he reaches me, he lowers himself to my level. I still don't want to look at him, but I feel him place his hand on the crown of my head. I close my eyes and I feel him press his lips to my forehead.

"May God forever bless the rhino keepers," I hear Chiku mutter from a short distance away. And then she falls silent, because there is nothing left to say.

THE HUNTED,
THE HAUNTED,
THE HUNGRY,
THE TAME

At the top of the world, the tundra is vast and the light is strange. Sometimes, it bends things until they transform. A distant seal can become the nose of a polar bear. The bear becomes an owl. The owl becomes a ship. The ship becomes a dog, and the dog becomes a wolf. And so on. But a whale is always a whale.

Bendiks awoke with snow settled over his paws and back, crystalline flakes of it clinging to his eyelashes. He stood and shook it from his body and it glittered in the long twilight of Northeast Greenland National Park. He was the first dog to wake that day. He had been dreaming in colors he had never seen before, and now, despite the spectacular landscape around him, the waking world seemed dim in comparison.

The long chain linking eleven dogs in a slumbering line began to rattle as the rest of them roused themselves. They stretched and shook the snow off. They yawned and began to whine for food. Bendiks looked around for Enok, the lead dog. It was, he felt, urgent that he speak with Enok about his dream. It wasn't just the strange colors. A whale had appeared, right before Bendiks woke, slipping through the deep beneath the ice where all of them stood. Bendiks looked down at his paws, worried that the whale had already swum from the water of his dreams and was circling below him.

"Enok," Bendiks said as he watched a man pause at Caris, the first dog on the chain, break off cubes of pemmican, and slip one into her mouth before depositing a pile right at her feet. Malthe was the man's name, and he stood before Caris, talking to her and running a hand along her flank before moving on to the next dog. All eleven of them were barking and still whining for food, and their breath whirled in clouds around Malthe and a second man, Villum, who had just emerged from a tent a short distance away. "Enok, are you listening to me?"

"I'm waiting for my food," said Enok. He looked past Bendiks toward Malthe and Villum, as they paused at each dog. Bendiks was the second-to-last dog in the feeding line, and Enok was after him.

"You'll be last," Bendiks said. "You have time to listen to me." Enok said nothing and kept staring, which Bendiks understood to mean that even if Enok did not care what he had to say, he would listen. "I had a dream last night. It was filled with new colors." Enok sneezed.

"What kind of colors?" Enok asked.

"I don't know. Different colors. Colors I've never seen before." Bendiks looked down and started pawing at the snow. He imagined that under the snow was a firm and thick layer of ice. And beneath that, the sea. And through the sea moved a shadow, swimming underneath all of them, waiting for them to move again so it could follow. "There was a whale." At this, Enok's ears turned and he looked at Bendiks, suddenly interested.

"What kind of whale?" Enok asked.

"A bowhead." Bendiks waited for Enok to say something else at this. To tell him what it meant for the whale to swim into his dream, but Malthe and Villum had reached them. Enok's tail started wagging as the two men came to their two last dogs, Enok the lone lead. The smartest, the strongest. Rational, steady Enok. And Bendiks, who came right after him in the swing position. Bendiks barely paid attention as Villum ran his hands along his head, leaned so close that Bendiks could see the frost in his beard, and whispered some encouragement about the day ahead. The pemmican tasted of nothing. Bendiks looked around the snowy expanse and thought about the times before when wind stirred up the snow around them, scattering the light, and wondered, if there was a whale, would the refraction multiply the whale into a hundred copies of himself? And if the whale was duplicated, would his duplicates all follow him? As he felt Malthe's hands fastening his harness, Bendiks repeated quietly to himself the things he knew for certain: *The ice is blue*, he thought to himself. *The ice is blue, the snow is white, and I am gray.* This comforted him, and he said it over and over to himself like an incantation, until he felt calm and ready for the day's journey patrolling the coast.

"Are you ready?" asked Enok, calling out to the line of dogs behind him, hitched to the sledge.

The ice is blue.

"We are ready!" called the dogs in unison.

"Where do we journey?" asked Enok.

The snow is white.

"We journey where our leader guides us!" called the dogs, now howling and jumping and straining against their leads.

"What is our purpose?" asked Enok.

I am gray.

"Our purpose is to run!" called the dogs.

"YAH!" Malthe's voice boomed out over the tundra as he and Villum pushed themselves forward on skis. Enok lunged ahead and the rest of the dogs followed. The sledge leapt to life and became not an inert thing but something like a serpent, moving swift across the landscape. The lines pulled taut and all the dogs moved as one, following the path that Enok set. The space was filled with the sounds of the dogs breathing, the rhythm of their feet on the snow forging a trail, the sledge rails skimming over the surface, and the slip of Malthe's and Villum's skis. Bendiks felt the cold air of the Arctic flood his lungs and travel throughout his body. It was as though a surge of electricity coursed through him and all he wanted to do was run. All he wanted to be was these feet racing across this snow, these shoulders pulling the sledge, this body moving in unison with the team on a journey up the coast.

And then, unbidden, another verse in the incantation rose up from somewhere in him and settled in his mind.

And the whale is black.

That night, the whale visited Bendiks again in his dream. The team had turned inland, toward the ice sheet, but in the second world of slumber, Bendiks dreamed that they were camping by the edge of the water in late spring, during the season of midnight sun, and everything glowed. The sea, gently lapping at the edge of the coast, appeared molten. Bendiks lifted his head and was overcome by the profound beauty of this incandescent day, and he struggled to understand why, until he realized that he must be seeing pink. He must be seeing orange. The sound of bowhead whales sending mating songs across hundreds of miles rang out around him.

One of them rose from the dark water out of nothing. His inky skin merged with the sea, except for his luminous white chin. The whale stared at Bendiks in silence until Bendiks's ears were filled with the pulsing of his own heart. He raised his head to try to catch the scent of the rest of the pack, only to discover he was on an ice floe, alone in the middle of the Arctic. The glow of the forever day subsided into polar night faster than it ever had in his waking life, and Bendiks saw that the chain that always kept him tethered to the others extended off the edge of the ice floe and into the sea. He was uncertain whether he was now chained to nothing or, more terrifyingly, chained to the whale.

"What do you want from me?" he asked the whale, trying to stare him down.

"To eat you," the whale said. And then he plunged under the surface of the water.

In the morning, after they were tied to the sledge, Bendiks stood next to Caris, shifting uneasily and whining to himself.

"What's wrong with you?" she asked. Caris was young and new to the team, but she stood next to Bendiks in the other swing position because she was confident. And she paid attention to everything. Bendiks looked at her and saw that her fur was bristled and she was alert.

"Nothing," he said.

"You're talking to yourself."

"It's nothing."

"I'm going to tell Enok you're talking to yourself. You shouldn't be up here if you're like that." Caris let out a howl. "Enoooook!"

"No, Caris!" Bendiks looked around, desperately but also fruitlessly because he was already chained, and wouldn't be able to run anywhere anyway, since the tundra was just an open and exposed stretch of snow that appeared to be endless. Enok was not tethered to the sledge yet and was a short distance away playing with Villum. When Caris howled, he turned abruptly and trotted over to them.

"Yes?" Enok asked, staring intently first at Caris, and then Bendiks. Bendiks knew how much Enok liked having these last moments with Villum before they started the day's run, and how this interruption would make him irritated.

"Bendiks is talking to himself," Caris said. "I don't think he should be swing today."

"I'm fine," Bendiks said. "I'm fine where I am."

"What's this?" Enok asked, either impatient or concerned. "What were you saying?"

"I couldn't hear him clearly," Caris said. "Something about a whale." Enok's ears stood up. Suddenly, Bendiks had all of his attention.

"What were you saying?" Enok asked.

"The whale's coming to eat me," Bendiks bent his head down and whispered at his own chest.

"I can't hear you," said Enok.

"The whale is coming to eat me," Bendiks said a little louder, talking as though his mouth was still full of pemmican.

"What?"

"THE WHALE IS COMING TO EAT ME!" howled Bendiks. The entire team stopped the shifting and playing and barking that had been going on among them, and all turned to stare at Bendiks. Enok was quiet. His eyes darted from Caris to the team and back to Bendiks.

"The whale," he said, "the whale from your dream." It was not a question.

"Yes."

"We are on the ice sheet now, Bendiks."

"Yes."

"The ice sheet is landlocked."

"Yes, I know."

"There is nothing under this ice but bedrock!" Enok growled.

"The whale can come in," Bendiks whispered again.

"HOW? How can a whale come in here? Into this desolate place?" Enok looked around to indicate the whole of the ice sheet. "Are you infected with permafrost?" Enok was now close to Bendiks's face, his breath swirling around both of them. "Is the diminished sunlight making you sick?"

"A whale can come in through the glaciers." Bendiks hadn't wanted to respond at all, he'd wanted to swallow the words, but they surged out like bile and he couldn't help himself.

"A WHALE CAN WHAT?"

"AglacierislikeapassagewayanditletsthewhaleinIdon't know," Bendiks exhaled the words like a deep breath. And once they were out, he knew they were true. And then Enok was at his ear.

"Stop it," he growled low, so that only Bendiks could hear him. "There is no such thing as a whale under ice." Bendiks said nothing. Enok never talked about dreaming anything. He couldn't understand.

"Watch him," Enok said to Caris. "Make sure he doesn't do anything stupid."

"Should he still be swing?" Caris called after Enok as he walked away.

"He's a strong dog," Enok called over his shoulder.

Throughout the day's journey, Bendiks was careful not to talk to himself. He turned when Caris turned. He kept the pace that Enok kept. Even when his paws hurt or his lead chafed his skin, he did not falter. And he journeyed where their leader guided them.

When Bendiks dreamed of the whale again he was no longer adrift in the middle of the ocean. And yet, he was alone once more. This time he was curled up in the center of the ice sheet. In his dream, the meltwater that snaked across the surface carving deep blue caverns had frozen again. The turquoise rivers slowed to nothing and the ice infected everything. Bendiks, wakened inside the dream, felt the ground tremble somewhere below. The whale was trying to break through. He closed his eyes, hoping to will himself away into a dream inside the dream. Someplace away from the ice sheet, someplace warm, someplace he had never been, with new colors and no chains. The ice trembled again. Then it crumbled. Chunks of it flew into the night sky launched by something he couldn't see. The whale's head emerged a few feet from his own.

"What are you doing here?" Bendiks asked, unable to speak above a whisper.

"I've come for you," the whale said.

"There is no water under that ice," Bendiks said, desperate to impress upon the whale that he didn't belong there.

"I can swim through stone," the whale said.

"I don't understand," said Bendiks.

"I can follow you," said the whale. "I can follow you wherever you are. And I can lead you."

"I have a leader," said Bendiks. "Enok is the leader. I follow him."

"If you follow me, I can make you the leader instead." The stone flowed around the whale like water as he swam in a wide arc around Bendiks. And Bendiks began to imagine what it would mean to be at the front of the pack. He would eat last, of course. And he would not complain. A good leader, a kind leader, thinks of the others and is content to eat last. Bendiks saw himself on a midnight-sun day, casting his gaze over the line of dogs, proud of their fortitude during the day's run. Satisfied as he watched their hunger be slaked first. He would be noble, of course, and he would not see it as suffering if the snow and ice caked in his paws sat a little longer while he waited for the others to be tended to. And Malthe would look at him at the end of the line, and his heart would swell with the feelings that men have for dogs and he would break away from the middle of the line and collapse on his knees, embracing Bendiks. *You have been so strong today!* Malthe would be weeping, of course, overcome by it all. And Bendiks would lick the tears from Malthe's face, because it wouldn't be right for their man to have frostbite on his naked skin. And then Bendiks, the benevolent, the kind, Bendiks the self-sacrificing, would push Malthe away with his nose and send him back to the others, because it was right and good that the leader be cared for last. And Bendiks as the leader would always be right and good, and nothing like Enok, who doesn't notice anybody but himself.

"If you make me the leader, what will I owe you?" asked Bendiks.

"When it is time, you will let me eat you."

"What about the others?" asked Bendiks.

"I don't need the others if I have you."

"When will it be time?"

"You will know," said the whale, and then he dove back into the bedrock and swam away.

In the morning, Bendiks woke and listened hard for the whale. He arrived during morning feeding, a shadow hovering under Bendiks's feet as he gulped his pemmican, grateful for the way it would nourish him for the day.

"I'm ready to follow you today," Bendiks whispered at the ground when he bent to pick up a new mouthful.

"Good," said the whale.

"Who are you talking to?" asked Enok.

"Nobody," said Bendiks.

"Nobody? I heard you talking. You said 'follow you.'" Enok glared at Bendiks.

"It's you. I will follow you today," said Bendiks.

"Good," said Enok. "Go where your leader guides you."

"I will go where my leader guides me," said Bendiks.

Wind blew across the tundra lifting snow into a fog that whipped around the team. Their breath froze into mist and they all struggled to see the path forward. They stood waiting as Enok sniffed the air, listened to the wind, and looked for the way.

"Are you ready?" Enok called to the other dogs.

The ice is blue.

"We are ready!" the dogs howled in answer.

"Where will you journey?" Enok called out.

The snow is white.

"We will go where our leader guides us!" called the dogs.

"What is our purpose?" Enok cried out into the wind.

I am gray.

"Our purpose is to run!" they all answered into the wind.

"Forward!" yelled Enok.

And I will follow the whale.

Enok lunged forward, and the team sprang to life in unison. Bendiks felt the thrill of beginning a run and he soon settled into a rhythmic pace. He matched his stride with the others as though they ran with one purpose and one mind. Enok was confident about their path. He surged forward with strong shoulders shouting commands to the line behind him. They all followed Enok, even Malthe and Villum.

But this was a devilish day. The fog thickened and began to obscure even the closest things. Bendiks could usually see Enok's tail and back feet as he ran out in front, but they began to vanish periodically, as though Enok was dissolving into an apparition.

"Are you there?" Bendiks asked the whale.

"I am here," said the whale. He was underfoot, swimming below Bendiks. Ready to whisper at him and guide him along the way.

"I can't see where we are going."

"You're following the coast."

"I can't see anything," said Bendiks, "and if I can't see, Enok can't see either."

"I will guide you," said the whale. "There is a cliff ahead. If you go too close to it your men will fall. You will all need to veer away."

"Enok will see it," said Bendiks. "He is our leader. His purpose is to lead."

"He may not see it," said the whale.

Bendiks strained to find Enok's feet in front of him. The chain that connected them led straight out in front and there was no slack in the line that would show that he was preparing to bend their path. "I don't know if he'll see it," Bendiks finally admitted.

"I'll tell you when you need to turn," said the whale.

"Can I trust you?"

"No more or less than you can trust your leader," said the whale. The team moved steadily forward, until Bendiks felt a change in the air, something suggesting an open space.

"Turn," said the whale, "there is a sharp drop-off coming." Bendiks, still positioned in swing, pushed hard to the right and felt Caris, tethered right next to him, resist at first.

"Caris, turn with me!" Bendiks said, low enough so only Caris could hear.

"Bendiks, that's not the way!"

"Trust me," he said. Caris looked at him, looked at Enok, and then turned with the same urgency as Bendiks. The other dogs followed and Enok was wrenched off his course with the rest of the team.

"Everybody stop!" growled Enok. The line of dogs abruptly stopped and the sledge skidded sideways until coming to rest against a small berm of snow. The dogs stood at attention, their muscles quivering, waiting for what might come next.

"Good," said the whale. "The edge is just beyond that berm."

"I saved them," said Bendiks. "I saved everybody." He turned to find Enok, so he could tell him that there was an edge, but by following the whale, he had kept them all safe. They were safe. But Enok stood with his legs planted firmly in the snow, his tail straight out and his ears pressed against his head.

"Move," Enok growled.

"No," said Bendiks. He could tell the coast loomed near and he could smell the ocean water.

"Bendiks, I am your leader. You go where I lead you, and you must follow."

"I am following the whale."

"There is no whale!" Enok, infuriated, lunged at Bendiks with his teeth bared and nearly clamped his jaws around Bendiks's neck before he was yanked back to the snow by Villum's firm hand pulling back his chain.

"Enok," Bendiks said, desperate, "there is a precipice there. We can't go forward. We must avoid the edge."

"There is no edge," he snarled. "You are imagining things. Move forward!" Enok bellowed at the team. The rest of the dogs, intimidated by the rage simmering in Enok's body, started to turn.

But Bendiks stood unmoved. The others piled up behind him; there was a snarl in the back. The clamp of a jaw. Bendiks looked back and saw a blur of fur and something spotting the snow. He smelled blood. And still he did not move.

"Move." Enok stepped close to Bendiks and bared his teeth. Drops of his saliva hit Bendiks's face and froze.

"Stay still," said the whale, swimming underfoot. And Bendiks was still. Snow and fog and their own breath obscured everyone's vision. Bendiks couldn't see more than a few feet ahead. And he felt suddenly as though he was surrounded by apparitions. All the other dogs that came before. All the other men. The other whales.

"Bendiks!" Malthe called out. "Go ahead. Bendiks, move forward."

And still he wouldn't move.

"Ya!" Malthe called.

When Malthe moved ahead of the team, his skis sliding silently over the snow, Bendiks was frozen. Fixed in place. Useless. He could not stop him. And this was something the whale had not prepared him for. That he would know the way. That he would try to guide them to safety. And that it would mean nothing.

Malthe approached the edge, blind as they all were from the swirling snow, and in an instant, it swallowed him.

He fell.

When Malthe's head went over the edge, Enok's eyes darted to Bendiks.

"It is not my fault," Bendiks whispered to the ground. Perhaps to himself. Or maybe to the whale, if he was still listening.

Villum yelled something toward Malthe, but the wind carried it away before Bendiks could hear it. The dogs, suddenly aware that Malthe had disappeared, started howling.

"Everyone, move forward slowly," Enok said. They all stepped close to the edge still chained together, so they could look over it. So they could look for Malthe. Over the threshold there was a rock-strewn slope that swept down steeply to the coast. The fjords were just beyond. The air began to clear, and it revealed Malthe lying in the snow. The scent of metal reached Bendiks and he knew without thinking that Malthe was bleeding.

They all stared at him, urging him up with their eyes. Two or three of the dogs started to whine, but Malthe was too far away to hear them. He was struggling. He rolled onto his side and then pushed himself onto all fours, like one of the dogs. Bendiks could hear him breathing heavily. Malthe pulled himself halfway up and onto one knee and Enok turned to Bendiks. At first his eyes were kind, but then they narrowed and he turned to look again at Malthe.

Together, they watched him slowly rise. The leader that they all followed. Malthe reached down to his thigh and swiftly pulled his own knife out of his flesh. Blood seeped from the wound. Bendiks imagined that the blood would eventually freeze.

Earlier, Bendiks dreamed that he was already inside the belly of the whale. He was there with all the others that came before him. He was inside the oldest whale, and they spanned generations. Together they sailed through the ocean as though the whale was a ship on a journey to nowhere. They began at the top of the world, made their way to the other end and back again. Inside the whale, it was as though time never passed. None of them grew older. None of them died. More and more generations joined them. They curled up together and they fought each other. The days ran together until they all stopped counting them.

There was no leader.

In this dream, the whale's back was transparent. When night came, they rolled on their backs and watched the stars. Sometimes they saw the northern lights. When they reached the southern tip of the world, Bendiks saw the southern lights for the first time. Something warm curved across the dark sky and he thought it was like the fibers of his unraveled lead. Like a ghost. *Is this red?* he asked the others. *Do you see that? Can you tell me, is it red?* But none of them knew the answer. Curtains of light rolled from one end of the horizon to the other. Bendiks imagined old dogs gripping torches in their mouths and running across the sky to light the way for the ones still pulling sledges. But it didn't really matter. Inside the whale, there was no snow. No chains, no sledges, no gear, no leaders. No cliffs. And no falls. Inside the whale they were all immortal.

Malthe climbed up the slope. Slowly, he returned to the team, breathing heavily. A strip of fabric was tied around his leg and there was snow caked on his hat. He carried his skis up over the edge all on his own. Villum called out to him and Malthe said something in reply, and when they came together, Villum took Malthe's arm and helped him step over the last berm before reaching the sledge.

Malthe refastened his skis and took up the leads, moving slower than usual. He shifted his injured leg forward like it was foreign to him, like he was passing it through a body of water. Bendiks could still smell his blood.

"It was not my fault," Bendiks said, when they stopped for a short rest. Malthe had stepped off his skis to retie the fabric around his thigh. Bendiks kept his tail tucked between his legs and crept close to Enok and tried to lick his teeth. Enok swiftly turned his head away and growled.

"What is your purpose?" asked Enok.

"To run," said Bendiks.

"Then why didn't you?"

Bendiks looked at the ground beneath him, hunting for a shadow. He wanted to ask the whale why things had become this way.

"Was it a trick?" he whispered to the ice. "I tried to save them."

"It wasn't a trick," came the whale's answer, though to Bendiks, it sounded far away.

"You lied to me. I'm not the leader."

"But I led you where you needed to go," said the whale.

Bendiks looked out against the darkening sky. The light had been fading gradually for days and as Villum refastened his harness to the lead, Bendiks found himself wishing for a longer rest. For quiet. For some distance from these other dogs who did not trust him.

They moved slower than usual to their next camp along the coast. Enok led and Bendiks followed dutifully. But he did not feel the pulse of electricity run through him anymore. He did not want to run. The ice beneath him was shadowless and empty as though the whale had left him behind.

When the polar night finally descended, and Malthe and Villum began to tether each dog to a chain for a period of rest, Bendiks dodged their hands and evaded their grasp. And to Bendiks it felt as though they didn't try to keep him, and he thought that perhaps they understood where he belonged. He ran instead to the edge of the land where it met the water. *Am I ready?* he thought to himself. *I am ready.* Cold air rushed into his lungs. *And where will I journey?* He looked out at the dark water, the surface undulating as though it was alive. *I will go where the whale will guide me.* Bendiks dove then, into the sea, to let the whale consume him. To let the ocean overtake him. He would become immortal. As the water embraced him, he understood that the others had not seen him plunge into the water. But later, they would know that he was there, slipping through the deep beneath the ice. A monolith. A leviathan. A zeppelin.

THE OPEN OCEAN IS AN ENDLESS DESERT

In all the sea, there is none more beautiful than my beloved.

She and I were born on the same day, so my mother says. In the warm waters, in the calving season. We were meant to be together, so my mother says.

But I didn't pay attention to my beloved during my early years. I thought only of my mother, and of staying near to her. I was her shadow and I swam where she swam; dove when she dove.

But this season, when my mother and I traveled to the cold waters, I found myself wanting to swim on my own. I was returning from a dive toward a trench in the ocean floor; my throat was full of water, the pleats stretched like a balloon. I had slowed down to press the water through my baleen when I heard the sound of the most exquisite whale emerge from a kelp forest. The fronds parted and her long form curved in to the open water. The water slipped over her like a sustained note and I heard her fluke flip toward the sky as she took a deep breath and angled toward me as if preparing for a krill dive. And I recognized her and remembered that I knew her.

"I love her," I tell my mother now.

"Why do you love her?" my mother asks.

"It's the slow way she moves," I say. "The way the krill drift and scatter around her. The way her fluke turns with her."

"Then you should travel to the warm waters with her," she says.

"But what about you?" I ask.

"I know the way," she says. "And we'll all gather together when you arrive with her."

"But I don't know the way."

"Listen to the songs. The songs always carry the route."

"Just the two of us by ourselves?" I ask. I'm nervous about traveling on our own.

"Yes. And you should sing to her," she says. "You should sing to her about the moon."

"Why the moon?"

"Because the moon song is what your father sang to me."

Fathers are the ones that sing the songs about our world. They swim away from everyone and send low notes through the water about where the krill is, where the temperature changes, and what the surface of the floor is like. They sing songs that tell everyone when to migrate. They announce the birth of new calves, and they notify us when a whale dies. Every song begins with one whale, composing alone in a low rumble. He sends his first notes along the ocean floor until they reach the whales nearest to him. They repeat the song to the next nearest whales who repeat it again. This goes on until the song wraps the globe like a net woven with the sound of whales humming. I will be a father someday too; I hope soon. And so, I am listening carefully to how the notes are strung together in a series of unbroken threads. I am learning the old songs and planning the ones I want to add to the fabric.

There is a story of a family of whales who chose to leave the sea. After they left the water, they grew legs and strayed from the shore. These whales grew lighter on their legs and the sun dazzled them as they walked further from the sea. They sang songs still, but the songs meant something different and the sounds didn't travel as far. When they came back to the sea, they found the water had no magic for them anymore. It was unfamiliar. Our songs meant nothing to them. The surf crushed them and the cold rushed straight to their bones and sent them rushing and splashing back across the sand screaming with glee and terror. They didn't belong with us.

Now, every once in a while, others will try to follow them. They range into shallow water and let the waves wash them aground. They lie there, waiting for legs that never arrive. Their skin becomes parched, and their bodies collapse under the weight of the sky. They cannot be out of the ocean, but many of them are unable to return to the sea.

"If I left the sea and grew legs, would you follow me?" my beloved asks.

"I would."

"How would you manage if you were still a whale and I had become something else?"

"I would wait for legs of my own. Or suffocate under the collapse of my own body."

"I am never leaving the sea." She says this every time she hears this story. I don't know whether I can say the same. I know almost nothing of life outside the water. Here with the dim light, and the increasing pressure, and the world all rendered in sound.

But we are together for now. During the day we search for food, and we find it gathered in the water column. I remember the words from the song net telling us to skip the place that is three surface heartbeats from the back of the fin-shaped trench because it is empty now. We visit a few of the other places where we have eaten before. Some of them are empty, and some are not. When I find someplace new, I hum a low krill song into the current before I curve through clouds of it. "Swim two surface heartbeats past where the floating squid was last year, then dive down three deep heartbeats before coming up under the cloud." I listen to my song join the lattice around us and I feel proud. As I swim up under the cloud, the surface light appears to shimmer in an imperfect circle, as if it is trying to resolve itself into a full moon. The sea around me is a deep and dim blue, and as I rise toward the krill I think of a verse for my moon song. "Hmmm, hmmm, four heartbeats to the moon. Hmmm, hmmm." I take great gulps of the cloud and feel the crimson mist vibrating as it streams through my baleen. At night, after I have eaten, I drift near the surface, slipping in and out of sleep, the song net humming under me, whole and perfect and full of our lives.

When I wake, there is a tear in the musical network.

I discover it when I plunge nose first toward the seafloor to send a question song into the fabric of the web. I want to know the way to the warm waters, so I can take my beloved there. My question flows out in all directions and I listen for the answer, but when it comes to me, it's pierced in the center by a note that doesn't belong. It has no variation. It repeats in loud bursts evenly and sounds exactly the same every time. And it has torn the directions in two, ripping out the center, the most crucial notes that I need to find our way. I swim back to the surface where my beloved drifts.

"The song is missing something," I say.

"What's missing?" she asks.

"It's a turn. An important one."

"We can find our way," she says. But I don't know. This is my first season traveling to the warm waters without my mother. I wasn't paying attention before and I won't know the way without the songs.

"Come listen," I say to her, "there is a note." We dive together and wait for the song to bounce back to us. And there it is again. Torn in two places now. "Do you hear that?"

"What is that?" she asks, swimming in an arc and turning her ear to the sounds.

"I don't know." The note keeps repeating over and over. My head is starting to feel numb and I feel the surface of the world around me flatten as the same repeating tone blunts all the curves and ridges. If it keeps going like this, everything around me will look the same.

"I remember the way there," she says. "I can take us to the warm waters."

"Don't you need the song?"

"I can hear enough of it." My beloved flips her fluke and turns around. But I'm not sure. The note has changed the surfaces around me and I'm no longer certain that I'm facing the right way. The direction song is broken in five places now and I can't remember whether it says to swim nine surface heartbeats along the narrow trench and then turn, or turn across the trench and then swim twelve heartbeats.

"I'll wait for my mother," I say. "I want to make sure she finds her way." When I say this, I don't even know if I mean it. Maybe I'm worried about my mother and don't want to swim without her. Maybe I'm afraid of getting lost. Maybe I don't believe my beloved knows the way. As I listen to her recede from me, the sound of her body gliding through the water becomes just a gentle noise in the background. I wonder whether this means I don't truly love her. But I've said that I will wait for my mother, and if I don't, does it mean that I don't truly love her either? And so here I stay for a while, drifting in almost one place, looking for neither of them.

Sometimes I wonder what the moon would look like from the land. And if the arrival of legs could take me up mountains. If they would bring me close enough to the moon to touch it. Would I have hands to touch it with? And if so, would I be able to reach out and grasp the hand of my beloved, if she, too, had traveled to the top of a mountain on legs that came after leaving the sea? Would she let me take her hand now that I'm no longer following her?

What we know about mountains on land is that they were carved from the trenches in the ocean floor and upturned far from the shore. They were made that way to remind the family of whales that left where they had come from. I think to myself that this means they live in an ocean in reverse.

My mother has not arrived. Should I stay and wait for her? Does she need me? I remember all the different times she took me to the warm waters and how she never got lost. If my mother doesn't need me, and my beloved doesn't need me, what does that mean?

I can't stay here alone forever, so I swim two heartbeats down and sing another question song. The answer returns to me uninterrupted and I turn in the direction my beloved swam, once again following her to the warm waters.

I remember from last year that this journey is long and I don't want to reach her as a weakened whale. So after swimming for fifty upper-water-column heartbeats I angle myself to the floor and plummet while I think again of my beloved. When I see her, I'll tell her that I'm sorry. That she was right. That she knew the way and I should have followed her. When I reach the center pressure point in the second water level below the surface, I find myself in the company of a giant squid. She is drifting in the water column in a hanging pattern and her tentacles are relaxed and pointed toward the seafloor. She is alone. I curve around her in a wide arc and turn my body back to her. I hear her eye move as it follows me.

"You won't eat me," she finally says.

"Is that a question?" I ask.

"No."

"How do you know?"

"You're baleen," she says. "You can't fit me in that mouth of yours, big as it is." The eye moves again. Evenly. I am aware of the beak that she keeps hidden. I haven't known a squid to use their beak on a whale like me. And yet, I have never trusted a squid.

"Your young would fit," I say. I can't tell anymore whether I am tracking the eye or it is tracking me. I keep turning.

"But I am not young."

"True." Her tentacles wave ever so slightly as she turns. I wait for the beak. "And you will not eat me," I say. This is also not a question.

"I don't eat baleen," she says. "I'm here waiting for whales to pass through." And it is this, her waiting, that makes me suspicious.

"Speak, squid." I curve around her again. "What do you want?"

"Are you going to the warm waters?" she asks.

"Yes."

"Don't," she says. "Don't go. Turn away. There is nothing for you there."

"There is everything for me there," I say. "I am going to sing for my bride." I roll in a slow spiral and turn again. "I am going. My family is going. All of the others are going. This is what we do every year. My song is ready and I will sing it."

"If you even have a bride to sing to," the squid says.

"I don't have any patience for your mysteries," I say. I feel my heart pulse inside my body and move my blood, thicker than the water around me. I think of how I heard that giant squids have three hearts: one for love, one for betrayal, and one for lies. And I don't know which one is beating for this squid right now.

"Don't all you baleens live slowly?" she asks. "Don't you have all the time and patience that was squeezed out of the rest of us by this ocean?"

"Deliberately, not slowly," I say. "There's a difference."

"Do you know about the nomads?" she asks. I hear her eye tracking me again. "The wandering sperm whales?"

"I do."

"The nomads lost six calves to them this year."

"Who is 'them'?" I am growing tired of this. I need to practice my moon song. And all this waiting with the squid is putting me farther and farther from my family.

"Them, they, it. It doesn't matter. You know what I mean. That noisy blade."

I turn and say nothing. I don't want the squid to know I don't understand.

"The ship. The ship!" says the squid, frustrated. "It only sings that one note. It crushes all of the sounds."

The note! The note that made me lose my way and pressed down on my head and wiped away my understanding of the world. The note that slashed the lattice of our songs to tatters. It made it harder for all of us to find each other. It was a ship.

"Six calves? You must be relieved." I didn't want the squid to know I was shaken.

"I know what it means," she says. "I'm not safe." I curve around her one last time and propel myself away from her. "It's coming for you, baleen!" she calls as I swim away.

I set off on my own again toward the warm waters. I sing another question song, and listen hard for the directions again. I want to get my bearings one more time. But this time all that comes back to me is something that used to be a song but is almost nothing now. There are great gaps now where the songs have been broken repeatedly by the note, and all I can hear are fragments. They are nonsensical songs like "swim six heartbeats to _____ over _____ cloud _____ krill _____ calving isn't," and they don't help me find my way to anything.

I feel now that I must find my beloved. The moon doesn't matter, my song doesn't matter. I need to find her. So I hum to myself, not to any other whale, but just to the world around me. It's just an ordinary ocean song. I hum it until I can hear the shape of the seafloor below me, the distance to the nearest trenches, the temperature of the water. I keep humming as I swim toward the warm waters, until I can hear the water move off the flukes of whales in the distance. They are all singing in chorus. It's a song about how they have arrived, and they're calling out the names of the whales that are already there. Old friends, family members. My mother is there. The sea around me is rich with creatures. Life blooms at the surface. Three gray whales slip by me, humming a warning song about an orca. I can hear the coastline and shape of water as it presses itself against the shore over and over. Small fish dart in and out of the coral gardens that ring the islands bursting from the sea. And I hear the sound water makes as it slips along the body of my beloved. I can hear everything. Everything!

And then.

And then.

It arrives.

ICHE ICHE ICHE ICHE ICHE ICHE ICHE ICHE ICHE.

The note, the ship, returns. And it grinds out the detail of the world. As the sound fills every drop of the water around me, the lush world I have just come to disappears. The trenches fill, the coral crumbles, there is nothing, and I am alone, suspended and directionless in an empty chamber. I turn to swim one way and send out a few notes to see where I am, but all that comes back is the flat surface of ICHE ICHE ICHE! I turn the other way and sing more notes. ICHE ICHE ICHE ICHE! Every direction is the same. I can't reach the song net anymore, and I feel as though, if I don't find it, I will be stuck here forever. But here is nothing left of it. If I want a song net, I must weave a new one.

I will have to travel to weave the lattice, but I don't know where I am so I just choose a direction. And the one I pick is right in front of my nose.

I charge forward through the water column singing only one short song now. I sing loud and at every frequency I know, at every frequency I can reach with my voice.

And my song says only one thing.

"THE NOTE IS A SHIP. THE NOTE IS A SHIP. THE NOTE IS A SHIP."

I race three heartbeats forward blaring my song into the sea. Then I dive one heartbeat, turn right, and swim for six heartbeats singing it still.

Turn again. Four heartbeats. Sing. Turn. Eight heartbeats. Sing.

Turn. Heartbeat. Sing. Turn. Sing.

TurnSingTurnSingTurnSing!

The whole of my body is spent and still I sing. Until everywhere around me is an intricate netting of "THE NOTE IS A SHIP!" I am fighting its sound. I am desperate to drown it out. But looming even louder is ICHE ICHE ICHE ICHE. I feel as though I will be hunted by it forever. I think maybe I want it to devour me, if that is the only thing that will stop this sound, this wretched note.

But when it bursts finally into my vision, I am not prepared. It's worse than anything the nomad was able to describe. Monstrous. Enormous. It skates at the surface like a giant blade slicing the sea, and I have only moments to pivot to the deep for a dive. One heartbeat. Two. I think I am safe when I feel something crash into my fluke and I'm sent wildly off course. My balance dissolves and I can no longer tell whether I'm diving, or swimming parallel to the seafloor, or turning, or spiraling anywhere. I smell blood. I don't know if it's mine. And all I hear is the ship. I try to still myself and listen. To find my place in the water. I sing a few notes. Slowly a picture returns. The seafloor appears in relief and gently rolling sand below me. I am in the lower middle of the water column. The ship is above me. Gliding as though I wasn't even there. I listen longer; the sound of it starts to diminish as it moves past me. And finally, it recedes.

I start to hum a song. Nothing special, just a hello song. Quietly, and then louder as I send it on a voyage along the curves of the sea. It reaches the coastline and travels into the crevices of the coral. It skates along the floor and sweeps up to the edges of the islands that rise up around us. When I surface for a breath and then submerge myself again, I hear my own song echo everywhere around me. I sing until everyone in this ocean knows that I am here, that I have survived. And then I wait. I am terrified that I'm alone. That the others were pummeled by the ship. That I, like the nomad, will return to the cold waters by myself with no beloved. That I will never be a father. But then the answer songs begin to wash over me. *I am here.* One whale. *I am here.* Two. And then three. And then three more. My mother. Enough for a pod. *I am here.* Four more. And then one more answer, different from the others. More of a question than anything else. *Tell me,* comes the song, *have you brought me the moon?*

A LEVEL
OF TOLERANCE

On the last day of my life, time becomes a thing that bends back on itself in an infinite loop and the day repeats itself in uncountable variations forever.

Sometimes I wonder if I have been dying for years.

The day begins.

I wake in my den. The dawning light filters through the tree roots at the opening where I first began digging in summer, four seasons ago. From where I lie, I can see the base of a few trees in our grove. I angle my head toward the opening and sniff the air. It is clean. Icy. It snowed last night. I turn back to my sleeping pups. They are warm and I count them to make sure they are all still there. That their hearts are still beating. I gently nudge them each with my nose. One. Two. I don't mean to wake them. Their fur is soft and it sticks out from their tiny bodies, piled together. They are so tangled that I can only tell them apart from the shades of brown, gray, or black in their coats. I lick two of them on the tops of their heads. They smell like the leaves that have drifted into our den. Like the flowers I find in summer. Three. Four.

I have woken them.

The little black one and the dark-gray runt look at me, blinking slowly. They start whimpering and sniffing the air. They wriggle together. They are looking for their uncle who has been missing for several days. He left for a rambling walk and never returned.

I have promised to search for him. Today, I will go over the Low Ridge, along the River, and toward the Road. I haven't been able to find him in all the usual places. Not in our old family den, the one where he and I had been raised as pups. Not in the cluster of brush where we sometimes wait for bison. Not behind the Ridge. I haven't seen his footprints on our route and all his markings have become aged.

Every morning, I check the snow near our den to see whether he has left any new tracks. Every day there is nothing. I don't understand. It's as though he has been lifted out of our valley by an invisible claw.

I have been avoiding the Road. It is a hideous black gash that rips open my valley. It frightens me, but my brother has been missing, and I must find him.

I move quietly away from my pups. For the past several days, I have sent my mate to go hunting with the pack instead of going myself. I don't want him to follow. I want someone to stay behind to provide for our pups in case I go missing too.

When I leave my den, it is still twilight. There is a blanket of clean snow on the ground, and my breath swirls in clouds. Our den is nestled in a grove of aspen and cottonwood trees. They are leafless and stark against the morning sky. A thin film of frost on the trunks catches the very beginning of the sunrise.

The grove glitters. I imagine my brother disrupting the quiet with his uneven trot. Tongue lolling out the side of his mouth. Impish. Like a pup. I close my eyes and picture him pausing in front of me, forelegs splayed awkwardly, his tail whipping back and forth in a playful rhythm. I almost want to wag my own tail to show him that I'm ready to leap into the snow with him, just in case. But when I open my eyes, the morning is still.

I step out of the opening and my paws sink softly into the powdery snow. It is dry, and today will be cold. I check the snow immediately around my den. I step carefully so that I don't disturb any tracks that aren't mine. There are only a few. My mate's and two others'. But there are none that belong to my heavy, gentle brother.

I take my usual route first, trotting through it quickly.

Ridge.

Cluster of Brush.

Old Den.

Rock Pile.

Today I must find him. I turn sharply toward the River. There is a tributary that breaks off in a fork where I often reach the bank to drink. I know if I follow this turn it will lead me to the Road. As much as I hate the Road, I love the River and its branches. The bison drink there and no matter what time of year it is, the River hypnotizes me. Today, the snow reaches all the way to the edge of the riverbanks. It is piled in rounded white domes on top of the boulders dotting the water's path. Narrow, leafless trees watch over the River in clusters. The world is severe and cold. And yet, the water flows. I could watch its rippling surface for hours. But not now. My brother needs me.

When I reach the split in the River, I pause to look at the mountains that cradle my valley. They surround me like a great craggy ring. They rise up like giants, draped in snow and dusted with trees scattered over them. Their immovable peaks comfort me somehow. I lift my nose to see whether I can smell my brother anywhere. I howl our song, hoping that he will answer me. One long, cascading call and four short ones. Then a long one again. We made this song when we were pups and still sing it to each other, even though everyone else has moved on.

I hate howling when I am afraid that no one will answer.

When I reach the Road, the sun is high overhead. I walk slowly in a crouch, keeping my belly as close to the ground as I can. The Road has a strange odor that sickens my stomach. Pungent and overpoweringly caustic. I shake my head, hoping to rattle the stench loose from my nose. I don't know what I will find here. There is something that catches the sunlight, nestled right in the crook of a bend in the Road. I can see its shape from the hill where I am crouched. For now, it is a gleam that stretches across the Road and strikes the snow. But I know the Thing is behind it. The Thing may have something to do with the reek of the Road, and I need to know what it is. There is a cluster of scrub brush up ahead, and I trot to it and crouch behind it to give myself time to figure out the Thing. I try to smell it and I can sense something different, but I don't know what. It is clean and sharp, an aroma almost like stone. I move closer. I make my way to a knot of four boulders and climb partway up on the center stone. The snow is so dry it falls away when I step into it. I stand tall, hoping to get a good view of the Thing that is catching the sun. A few seconds pass and a group of clouds drift over the sun, blocking its glare. The Thing is something that I have seen only once or twice. It is something I try to avoid. My mate calls it a Growler, for the noise he says it makes. But my brother said it is a Machine. And that it carries human Hunters.

Once, I was moving through my territory with my pack. We were stopping at all our usual spots, marking our boundaries, protecting our land. I remember I broke away for a while to track a herd of bison. And then there was nothing. I fell into a deep sleep beset with strange dreams. Something kept turning me over. Quiet murmurs came out of three or four looming, naked faces. I woke up alone in a grove of trees feeling strange with something around my neck. Later, my mate said that humans gave it to me. That he saw them take me away. That they were gentle when they returned me. It bothered me at first. I remember trying to tear it off, trying to back out of it. I thought it might be some sort of animal that would suffocate me, hoping to feed off me. But then I realized it was something else entirely. Harmless. It had a gentle hum that only I could hear. Now I don't even notice it anymore.

But Hunters are another thing. I have seen them only a few times, and I have always been afraid of them. They have the same naked faces from my dream, but they are rigid and silent. My brother never quite understood my terror. He has always been so curious about them. Sometimes I worry that he seeks them out. He says that they look weak. And helpless. He says they are hairless, which I know is true. They cover themselves with something that is like fur but not quite. The skin on their faces is so exposed. The first time he came back to our pack after seeing a Hunter, he kept marveling at how cold it must have been, how it might die in the winter. Even the Machine didn't scare him away. He used to dance in little patterns when he knew there were Hunters nearby. Rushing forward, then leaping back again. Wanting to see them, but knowing I didn't approve.

The day that I look for my brother, there are two Hunters that tumble out of the Machine. One is the size that I remembered from before, but the other is small. The smaller one looks so fragile. Its wrapping looks cumbersome, and it stumbles in the snow after it emerges. I think that maybe it is the Hunter's pup. I sniff the air. The big one smells earthy. Sweaty. Loamy. He works his jaw like he has something in his mouth. But I can barely smell the pup. Just the faint scent of something sweet. I can't tell if my brother is there. I need to get closer, but I'm afraid they might see me. This side of the Road is so exposed. Beyond the boulders, scattered brush, and some lonely trees, is endless snow. White and unmarked.

Later, the Hunter will refuse to be identified. He will say that I lunged after his pup. That he had to protect his boy. He will describe my teeth. The crazed look in my eyes. He will say that I was rabid. That the collar could be recovered and put on another wolf. That I didn't matter anyway.

His story will be a lie. Instead, I turn my head, thinking that out of the corner of my eye, I see a scrub jay, my brother's favorite bird. I want to ask the jay if he has seen my brother. But there is no bird. Only a trick of light.

And then there is sharpness ripping through my chest. And warmth spreading. And a sound that comes fast and echoes. I can't say which one happens first, the sound or the sharpness or the echo. And then the world tilts on its axis, and I can't right it, no matter how hard I try.

I imagine that time is a predator. That I have been Hunted. That I will be Hunted. That I am being Hunted.

The day begins.

I wake up from an arresting dream of an elk that I once hunted to feed my pack. It was mature and massive with antlers so large they reached out like the branches of a winter tree. I wanted to provide for my pack so I took it down on my own and then sang to my pack so that they would come and I could feed them. In my dream, I can feel the wind on my face as I run toward the elk, lifting up onto my toes, picking up speed. I can feel my jaw bear down; I can feel my teeth pierce through the elk's hide. I can feel the strange sensation of its coat on my tongue. I can feel the dull thud of my shoulder against ice when I bring the elk down and we slide across a stretch of frozen water. It feels so real that I can barely tell the difference between waking and sleeping. And yet, in my dream, my brother was with me. Dancing alongside on the snowy bank of the River. Celebrating that I could do something so difficult by myself.

And then I remember.

He is missing.

I am alone in my den with my pups. My mate has already left to hunt. My pups are still sleeping. I start to count them, careful not to wake them. One, two. They are warm and sweet-smelling. I can't help nuzzling into their soft, full bellies. Three, four. I wake them. They whimper. They are waiting for their missing uncle. I must find him today.

I have looked everywhere, but he is nowhere. I have looked everywhere but the Road. I check the Low Ridge again. The Brush Cluster. Our Old Den. The Rock Pile. I know he won't be there, but I can't help myself.

I am avoiding the Road. I know where it goes.

When I have exhausted all of our places, all of our extended homes, I follow the River to its fork and pause to sing our song, in case he is listening. Nobody answers. Not even the echo of my own voice. I follow the branch of the River that will guide me to the Road. I see its path over the crest of a sloping hill. Beyond scattered brush and a few boulders stretches a broad expanse of white. The Road is empty except for one Machine. The smell of it gnaws at me. The Unidentified Hunter emerges with a smaller one in tow. I am wary, but I need my brother.

He is a riverbank and I am the water rushing toward him.

I slink closer to the Road on my belly. I am gray and I know the Unidentified Hunter may see me against the unmarked white snow. But I am hoping that these Hunters are careless, or weak, or clumsy, the way my brother always believed them to be.

I dash behind a snarl of leafless winter shrubs and stay there. My breath creates a cloud of fog, so I slow it as much as I can. I watch the Hunters and the Road. The big one and his pup. They hardly move. Take only two or three steps away from their Machine. They pace in front of it. My brother was right. They are weak. Or if they are not weak, they are lazy. They

142

cling to the space around the Machine as though they will die without it.

I grow confident and move even closer.

The sun moves overhead and I crawl slowly. Even closer.

Eventually, the Hunter and his pup climb into the Machine. It swallows them through two openings, one on either side. The openings each have a little door that closes the Hunter and his pup inside a sort of den: the belly of the Machine. Once they are inside, I can't smell them anymore, but I can still see them. They have turned their backs to me. The Hunter reaches out a hand and places it on his pup's head.

The Machine has a trough attached to the back of the den. It is long and rectangular, with sharp edges. The sun reflects off it in strange patterns. I cannot see whether the trough is full or empty. I don't know whether it is full of water like a pond or full of something else. I start to imagine that my brother is in the trough, and then I can't think of anything else. I slink around behind the Machine, as low to the ground as possible. Low enough to remain unseen by the Hunter, but high enough to see what is inside the trough.

The angle is tricky, and I end up moving closer and closer until the only way I will be able to see inside is to climb into it. I can feel my heart beating faster than I am used to.

I can hear my own breathing.

I hope my brother is in there.

I almost know that my brother is in there.

I need to calm myself, but now I am obsessed with getting inside.

He is in the trough.

I can hear his breath.

It isn't my own; I am certain of it.

It is him and I have found him and I have rescued him and all I need to do is climb into the trough to show him the way out and then I can return him to our pack.

I will give him the first taste of my next kill.

I will make a new song with him.

I will send him into my den with my pups to rest.

All of this will happen as soon as I climb inside.

I can hear him whining.

It isn't me.

I am sure of this.

It is my brother and he knows that I am here.

I am a few feet from the trough. The Hunter still has his back to me. Now is my chance and I must leap. I ready myself for a jump. Coiled low. I imagine the den of the Machine as a great elk that I must take down on my own. And then I burst out of the white snow. It is one of my best vaults and I clear the nearest edge of the trough with no trouble and land squarely inside.

But I am mistaken.

The breath, it was mine.

The whining, it was mine.

The trough is empty.

There is no brother here.

It is too late when I realize the Hunter has turned around and seen me. He opens a transparent door at the back of the Machine's den and a narrow, long object emerges. There is the noise. And the echo. Then the pain and the spreading warmth and the whole world that I know turning and slipping away from me, while I lie alone in the empty trough far from my pack and my den.

Imagine that time is a spool of thread that the Unidentified Hunter clutches close to himself. Imagine that he unravels and rewinds it over and over again, undoing things that have been redone. Wolves. Then no wolves. Then wolves again.

The day begins.

I wake in my den counting my pups. I don't want to wake them, but as I burrow my nose into their warm bellies, they wake anyway.

I remember that I have been looking for their uncle.

I remember that I have had trouble looking for him at the Road. Is it because he has been there and I have missed him? I am not certain, so I decide that I will go to the Road to look for him one more time.

I know that he isn't at our usual places. He isn't at our old den. He isn't at the cluster of shrubs where he and I used to play as pups. I can feel his absence as something palpable, a shadow wolf following me everywhere I go. I follow the River until I reach the fork and then I sing our song halfheartedly, knowing that he won't answer. The valley spreads out before me. I can see the whole of our world. We are the lucky wolves, roaming in this beautiful place. When my brother and I were pups, he could not stop marveling at the limitlessness of our home.

"Why is the Sky so big?" he would ask me. "Why are we small? Why is there snow? Why does the River run in the

summer and slow in the winter? Where does the River go?
Why are there stars?"

When we were trotting after our mother, following her tracks
and trying to smell the hooved things as they moved through the
valley, my brother would be chattering the whole way, tripping
over his own feet and pointing out all the things I notice now.
These are the things that I see now that he is no longer here to
tell me about them: tufts of clouds, the gentle slope of the Hill
dropping down into the Valley, the curve of the River in summer,
the color of the brush we hide behind when we are hunting, the
hide of a great elk, and the smoothness of each individual hair.

One of my pups reminds me so much of my brother. The
two used to be inseparable. They sang new songs together.
When dusk had come and gone, I could still find them making mournful cries to nothing. Howling off-key to no one. My
brother and my little black pup were often roaming around our
territory asking each other questions and making up the answers. My pup wondered why snow can be sticky but also dusty.
My brother said it is because the snow cannot make up its mind.

Will my pup someday be missing like my brother? I don't
know.

I am lost in memories of my brother, so I don't realize how
much time has passed and suddenly the Road is right in front
of me. I see the Unidentified Hunter and his Machine only a
short distance away. The Hunter and his pup have their backs
turned to me. They are looking at something inside the den
of their Machine. I am feeling bold, so I walk toward them
without trying to hide myself. I want to ask them if they have
seen my brother. He limps, I will say. He trusts others. He isn't

a good hunter, but I love him anyway, I will say. Maybe all this time I have misjudged human Hunters. Maybe they will understand what it means when someone is missing. Maybe they will help me. I come up close behind the Hunter's pup, and I wait for him to turn around.

When the pup finally turns around, I ask him, "Have you seen my brother?" His face tells me nothing about my brother. He looks at the Hunter and they make sounds at each other, but I can't understand them. I move closer and try to describe my brother. Perhaps they don't know what he looks like. I tell them that he has a tuft of white fur on his chest. That three of his paws are black, but one is gray. But the pup backs away from me and won't listen. The Hunter turns back to the Machine's den, and the pup reaches into his jacket and pulls out an object. I have seen one of these before. My brother told me it is called *knife*, but to me it looks like a great tooth. I don't understand why the pup would need a tooth right now. There are no elk or bison nearby. There is nothing to eat. But he waves it at me just the same. I am fascinated. I can't stop staring at the tooth. I am still staring at it when the sound comes once again.

And then the echo.

Then a sharpness and spreading warmth.

The order is clear.

I don't understand why the Hunter has done this to me. I was only looking for my brother.

Imagine that time is a rifle. That time has a mechanism. That time is well oiled. That the Unidentified Hunter holds time in his hands.

Imagine that time is a knifepoint pressed to my heart. That time is our song that I sing to myself. Imagine that I am suffering.

Imagine that time is your eyes. That time is my pups. That time is our mother. That time is nothing, nothing at all.

Every day that begins, ends the same way. With darkness. With a tilting world that tips so far I slide off the edge into nothingness.

Oh, my brother, you have been missing for so long. I don't know where you have been, and though I have been searching, I can't find you anywhere.

The day begins.

LET YOUR BODY MEET THE GROUND

The way it was before, after night-rest on the edge of the roof of the tea stall, the sun would flood the sky with colors, and I would begin to calibrate my sun compass. As the dawn light brightened into day, it would filter down into the streets and alleys of the market in Chandni Chowk, like ink spreading in water. And from my home roost at the tea stall, lines would run out over the city showing me all the places I could fly to. I would take to the air and fly over and around Old and New Delhi, watching the lines change color to show me where I was going. Orange for my home roost. Pink for the roosts of my friends. Yellow for the cricket stadium where we would go to gather discarded food from crowds. Green to the water fountains. Blue to the metro stations. Violet leading to the forest on the other side of the river. Among all the tangled threads of my homing lines sat a tall red building with a courtyard, right next to the Lal Mandir. It is the Charity Birds Hospital.

It had been a place I'd only skimmed over when I flew around the city. My homing lines never led me to stop there, and instead flowed over and around the edges of the modest dusty red towers and the crimson rectangular building with a cage on top that rose up over a courtyard next door. The lines were usually muted, the color of charcoal or ash, and I never stopped there. I never stopped there until I had no choice but to be there.

It was where I met Toy Man.

Did you know that during the Kite Festival some kite flyers coat their thread in glass? Did you know that when the kite is high, the threads can sometimes curve and bend with the grace of a flowing river? Did you know that when the glass catches the light the thread can glow like homing lines? I did not know these things. Until I had no choice but to know these things.

What I mean to say is that during the Kite Festival, I followed a silver pink line that ascended in a soaring crescent and at its apex was a demon with enormous fierce eyes, wings spread to fill the whole sky, and a mouth open to devour me. I froze, unable to propel myself anymore with my wings and I tumbled backward into the thread, which was not a homing line at all, but was a burning knife that swiftly passed my feathers to lay its malleable blade on my skin. I fell and as I tumbled down the thread bent itself around my wing, burning deeper still. I tried to fly away and it gripped me like a snake, coiling around me. I looked up and saw that I was pulling the demon down with me. The demon's wings collapsed as the loft of the air gave way and we began a rapid descent together. I felt helpless. Powerless, as the sky spun around me. Unfamiliar and disorienting. At some point in our fall, the demon overtook me and it landed in the branches of a bush first and then I came after, the plant and the demon keeping my body from the ground. I thought at first the demon would take me away forever. And so I kept my eyes closed, waiting. Waiting for the pain in my wing to expand or subside and for whatever was next to come. But nothing happened.

I opened my eyes and I realized I wasn't in the embrace of a demon after all. It was the paper and frame of a kite. I looked around and couldn't see any birds I recognized near me. People rushed by on the street, brushing past the bush as though I wasn't there. I turned my head back and forth trying to catch the attention of someone, anyone. But I was alone. My wing was bound by the glass string and felt as if it was in flames. I looked up and opened my mouth to try to call out, but no sound would come. I saw the homing lines far above me glowing and lighting the way to all the places I could call home. And I couldn't rise to meet any of them. Do you know what a bird is without any guidelines? A bird like that is lost to the world. A bird like that will die in the place she has landed. These are the kinds of thoughts I had as I sat in the crumpled kite in the bush, unable to fly, bound to the earth with a burning thread, and closed my eyes to the sky.

When I opened them I was in a new place. I felt as if I had newly emerged from the egg again and had joined a new world. I was cradled in a pair of warm hands, with my feet facing the ceiling. A woman's face loomed over me and a curtain of dark hair hung around both of us, obscuring our surroundings.

"Hello, little kabootar," said the face, "I'm Dr. Shah." It was a strange feeling, being upside down in this way. But I didn't feel unstable the way I had in the sky. "Your wing is injured," she said as she took a strip of white material and wrapped it around my wing and my body. "The Kite Festival was exciting, wasn't it?" she kept wrapping. I wanted to tell her that it hadn't been exciting at all. I wanted to tell her about my homing lines. And the glass string. And how I felt I had become lost to a demon. But I didn't have any words that she could understand. So I just looked at her and this new place I was in. She had righted me and set me down on a piece of cloth on a counter inside a building and walked to the other side of the room. The counter was metal and cool on my feet when I stepped off the fabric. I stood in the light coming through a window. Beyond the window I saw a long row of cages lining a wall that was painted the color of a kingfisher's wings. I heard the gentle cooing of other pigeons and the twittering of other kinds of birds. I could smell feathers of all kinds. A sound pierced the room and I heard Dr. Shah's voice right after it stopped. "Hello, Charity Birds Hospital . . . Kyah? This is Dr. Shah. Haan, haan. You can bring it in. That's fine. OK. See you."

Charity Birds Hospital. I was inside. I was wounded. The others here must be wounded too. I remembered suddenly something I hadn't thought of before. Once when I was flying with the others on our way to the market, the normally gray lines around the hospital building were beginning to glow in green and blue. At the time we didn't know what to make of it. But then suddenly all the lines coming from the hospital exploded in a burst of color and seven birds emerged in exuberant flight from the cage at the top of the building. They didn't pause to circle and talk to us, but sailed away before we could stop them, away from the city, toward a forest in the distance. Those birds had been inside once. But at the end they were outside again. I didn't know whether I would ever be outside too. I knew it was what I wanted, but as I stood on the metal table, my wounded wing bound to my body, I realized that what I really was, was a bird with one wing. A bird with one wing cannot fly. A bird with one wing isn't a bird at all, but the echo of a bird. The memory of a bird. And the memory of a bird is really nothing at all.

And then Toy Man came.

Dr. Shah held me in her hands by the window again. She had just tipped me onto my back to find the end of my bandage when I heard the main door open, and then voices in the corridor, and then two sets of footsteps coming toward us. Dr. Shah set me back down on the table.

"Dr. Shah," said a young man, "I tried to tell him you were busy, that he should come back, but . . ." and an older man pushed his way past the young man. He had long thin legs and a belly that rounded out over them, tight like a drum. As he walked toward Dr. Shah he turned his toes out slightly. He walked like a bird. I liked him immediately.

"Beti! I've come to see your patients!" He reached his hands out to her and Dr. Shah walked forward and gripped them tightly.

"Hi, Uncle, you've arrived at the perfect time," she led him to my table. "This one came in yesterday. Her wing was tangled up in manjha at the Kite Festival." Dr. Shah leaned down toward me. "I need to change her bandages but she fidgets when I turn her over. Can you distract her?"

"Haan, haan. Of course, beti." He reached into a bag at his side, and started looking for something.

"OK, let me turn you," Dr. Shah reached out to me and gently clasped me in her hands. I felt her sweep me onto my back and she started tugging at my bandage, when the old man's face appeared above me.

"Little kabootar!" he said as his eyes widened so much that I couldn't tell whether he was shocked at my injuries or surprised because he had never seen a pigeon up close before. "I have something special for you!" He brought his hand out over me and hanging from it was a little figure made of beads and pieces of straw, all attached to strings. I blinked twice and then looked at them carefully and saw there was no glass on them. And then the man moved his fingers in a pattern and the figure began to dance! Was it alive? I didn't know, but it was wonderful! "This is a puppet, little kabootar. It's for playing like this." He made it dance some more. "It's a little toy I made." A toy. He made it. He was the Toy Man.

That day, as I lay in Dr. Shah's hands, I looked up at Toy Man's puppet, and almost didn't feel the pain in my wing. Or think about how I wasn't flying. Marvelous! I stared at him for a while, and then past the puppet to his face, and further still to a machine whirring from a spot on the ceiling, spinning inside a cage. I had not seen a ceiling from the inside before and thought how strange that the sky would stop like that, so low. Toy Man smiled down at me.

"Ah, you see the fan, don't you?" said Toy Man, as he made the puppet dance a little more above me. "It's in a metal box, do you see? But that's OK. It's OK. It's to protect you. When you are recovering and well enough to try flying again, the box will keep you from the blades." The puppet twirled and bowed at me in the air above.

"I don't know if she'll be flying again," said Dr. Shah. She turned me sideways and checked the bandage. "Her wing is very damaged. I don't know if she'll recover all the way."

"Ah, OK, OK." Toy Man looked confused, and the puppet was still.

"Don't worry, Uncle, she can live here if she isn't able to fly!" Dr. Shah patted Toy Man's arm, and holding me tucked in her palm, she walked back to the hall and put me in a cage in the middle. Newspaper pages were spread out on the bottom and there was a metal dish inside with fruit and seeds, and another with water. "If we can release them, we release them. But if not, we still try to save them and they stay here," she said as she shut the door, and pressed it so the latch clicked. The sounds of other birds preening, cracking open seeds, and tearing paper gently thrummed in the background. It was quieter than the city in here and the noise brought me some comfort.

"Ah, I see," Toy Man had followed Dr. Shah and was peering at me closely now through the mesh of my cage. I couldn't see the puppet anymore and I imagined it hung slack in his hand. I wondered if I would become like the puppet. If I was missing a wing. Toy Man looked at me quietly and then brought his hand up to the mesh of my cage. "I'll come tomorrow, little kabootar. I'll see you then." And he and Dr. Shah walked down the corridor toward the light of the doorway leading outside.

As I watched them recede from me, I realized I had seen Toy Man before. But I was used to seeing him from above, so it took me a while to recognize his face. He was the man whom I would see in the mornings at the Madras Coffee House or the tea stall, and who would throw little bits of food to us when we sailed down from the rooftops and gathered in the street. Then he would walk to the children's hospital before disappearing into the doors and emerging only hours later. He had hair on his face, and the sides of his head, but none on the top. On his walk he would stop every few minutes and pick up little things that he found. Bottles. String. Things like that. And he would tuck them into a bag slung over his shoulders. I would watch his head bob down and up as he found things and retrieved them.

When Toy Man came back the next time, he brought another thing to show me. It still hurt where my wing had been injured, and sometimes when I woke I didn't remember where I was, and when I tried to stretch my wings I remembered I was bound up and trapped, and the wounded wing nagged at me like a ghost. I felt as if I would always be stuck in here. I wouldn't ever be able to stretch that wing again. I wouldn't ever be able to fly. I would never go anywhere. Dr. Shah had placed a new pile of seeds and another pile of small pieces of fruit in my cage and I didn't want either of them.

"Dr. Shah says you aren't eating!" Toy Man's face loomed large at the door of my cage and he leaned close to peer in at me. "Look at what you have." His skin smelled like aftershave and lotion, and the parathas he must have recently eaten. "Star fruit! You don't like it? It's good. Shaped like a star, just like from your home . . . the sky." He pointed upward and winked at me. I didn't look up. I couldn't see the sky from here. And I wouldn't be in it anymore. "Yes, OK. Maybe no star fruit today. OK." Toy Man was quiet as he looked away and rummaged through the bag slung over his shoulder. "What if I made you a little something?" He produced a piece of a plastic drinking straw and a wooden pencil and displayed them to me. "You know these, yes? These are ordinary things. Now watch what I do." As he pinched the straw in the center, I walked right up to the door of my cage. I didn't understand, but I wanted to see what would happen. Then he carefully pierced the straw with the end of the pencil and rolled the wood between his palms. The straw spun around and around. "Do you see, little bird? It's a pinwheel! Like your fan." And he pointed again at the ceiling to remind me. I did see. And it was wonderful.

Toy Man came back the next day. And the day after that. And then he didn't come for three days and I sat in my cage turning fruit pieces over and over and trying to pull open the latch. I wanted to come out and walk down the corridor and out the door. I wanted to see the sky and my lines. I thought I would feel better if I could see the lines leading to my roost or the market. The latch was heavy and I knew from watching Dr. Shah that it needed a turn and a push. I had climbed the cross bars of the door and was gripping them with my feet. I had my good wing stretched a little for leverage while I pushed at the latch pin with my beak. I didn't think I would really be able to do it, but the door swung open with my feet still gripping it! It swung me right into the corridor and I could see all the way to the door. I saw Toy Man's birdlike silhouette standing in the sun-filled doorway. I flapped my Only Wing to try to swing the door back part of the way to my cage and after a few robust flaps it started to move.

"What are you doing?" asked the parakeet in the cage above mine. He had a bright magenta head and a brilliant green body and had been here longer than I had.

"Never mind," I said. I looked down at the cage below me. All our cage doors had thin bars in a grid. I carefully, one foot at a time, climbed down to the lowest point on my door. And then I flapped my Only Wing twice and hopped down to the door below me.

"You aren't supposed to open your cage," said the parakeet, more urgently now. "Where are you going?"

"I am out," I said as I climbed further down and hopped from the lowest cage door down to the cool tile of the floor. "I am going to see Toy Man." And I turned toward the corridor and away from my cage.

I walked past the exam counter by the cages, past Dr. Shah's swiveling chair, with the fabric surface that some of us like to pull threads from, and continued along the wall until I was close to Toy Man and could hear him and Dr. Shah speaking to each other.

"I understand, Uncle, I do. But I can't let you take her out." I looked at Dr. Shah, first at her feet and then I followed the tall tree of her body to her head. Her glasses had slid down her nose and as she pushed them up I saw a thread hanging from the cuff of her white coat start to move as if a breeze was sweeping by it. Maybe it was the fan, or a breeze from outside, but it made me think of wind and the way it felt on my feathers, and how I was beginning to have trouble remembering that feeling now.

"Beti." Toy Man gestured helplessly at her with his palm out. "Dr. Shah, please, I think it would be good for her. To see more outside. To see something that will remind her that someday things will be different."

"I'm sorry, Uncle, it's just not possible," said Dr. Shah.

"OK, OK, I understand." Toy Man was quiet for a moment and I stepped a little closer to him. I thought I saw him glance down at me, but when I looked once more, he was speaking to Dr. Shah again.

"Your children will like these," he said, pressing some small items into her hand. "And they are easy for children to make on their own if they want to. If you bring them sometime, I can show them."

"Thank you, Uncle, they'll love these." Dr. Shah smiled at him as he turned back toward the corridor leading outside. As he walked past me, he looked down at me one more time (he did look!) and he winked at me. I turned my head this and that way, but Dr. Shah was occupied, so I hopped down the hall after Toy Man.

He was lingering silently by the door. It was open and his body was a dark silhouette against the light of the world outside. I stepped close to him and he crouched down to the ground, leaning in toward me. His head became very large this near to me.

"Would you like to come on an adventure today?" Toy Man asked.

I blinked at him and looked back down the hall. I couldn't see Dr. Shah.

"Just outside." Toy Man pointed at the open doorway behind him. "Out there." He set his satchel down on the ground and opened the top flap. I thought about my Only Wing. And the lines leading to home. And the lines leading to all the places I had never been. And what it was like to fly and feel the wind up above this hospital, and this ground that I had been so close to these days. I thought also about how hard it was for me to pry my cage door open. And I hopped into Toy Man's bag.

Toy Man gently closed the flap of his bag and snuffed out the light. I nestled myself among his things and tried to imagine that I was back inside the shell of an egg. I don't remember what it was like but I think it would be something like this. Dark and enveloping, the sounds of the outside world filtered and muffled to something unidentifiable. And then I felt myself move. I felt the bag lift, with me in it, and swing freely before being pressed against Toy Man's side, his arm curved around me. I felt myself, us, begin to rock gently as he stepped forward out of Charity Birds Hospital and into the world.

I knew we had passed Jalebi Man's stall when I smelled sugar and frying oil. As Toy Man kept walking I heard the spin of bicycle wheels, people calling out to each other about prices, and family news, and who was eating and what they all wanted out of this world. Close and confined and compelled to listen in a way I had never been before. We were in the heart of the market.

And then Toy Man's pace slowed and he stopped and turned the flap of his bag open. Bright light flooded my eyes and I thought that this was not like what hatching would have been like, which probably happened slowly, after steady chipping away at the shell. All the sounds and smells that had been muffled before rushed at me. And then Toy Man leaned over and blocked out the sun with his head.

"Hello," he said, smiling widely. "Do you want to come out?" I stared at him. This was the second time I had been so close to Toy Man without a cage door separating us and I was still amazed at his size. I thought I understood now why people were so attached to the ground. Their heads looked so heavy. They would never be able to lift them far enough into the sky to see their own homing lines, if they even had them. Toy Man reached into his bag and swept his palm under me and lifted me into the open air of the street. In one smooth motion he swept me onto his shoulder where I settled with my wounded wing nestled right against his head.

He sat on a low stone wall alongside a park and brought me down on the stone to stand beside him. I looked up to the roof lines where I would have chosen to be before. And I watched other pigeons drop down to the street and then back up again. And I thought about what it meant for me, to be here on the ground, living my life beneath the lines that could guide me home. I looked up and could still see the threads glimmering above me, like a fine net. Like a living fabric. I wanted to return to it, but my Only Wing would not be able to take me there. I looked over at Toy Man and saw him focusing on a series of folded papers, quietly whispering something to himself. When he saw me looking at him, his eyes lit up again.

"Little kabootar, we have places to go today," he said. And then he tucked me back into his bag and I was once again hidden from the day. I liked the bag. It turns out that I was not alone inside it. There was a small notebook, a pen, things like strings, tabs from the tops of cans, and bits of a straw and a pencil, like what he used for the pinwheel that he made for me. All things that smelled like the streets, and the market, and Toy Man's hands.

Through the fabric of the bag I heard the voice of a woman float through the air of the train announcing Rajiv Chowk Metro

Station as the next stop. Toy Man stood up, pushed through to the door of the train and gently patted the side of his bag where I was nestled. He gathered the bag in his arms to protect me from the crush of people and we made our way out to our next adventure.

Toy Man walked up the stairs from the metro station and when we emerged into the sunlight, he took me out of his bag and lifted me back onto his shoulder. We were now in an open area, quite unlike the market where I was roosted and where Charity Birds was nested. Toy Man stood uncertainly on the pavement as though suddenly he had lost sight of all his plans.

A rickshaw whizzed by and Toy Man jumped, almost sending me tumbling down from his shoulder. He reached a hand up and I felt his warm palm against my body.

"OK," said Toy Man, to no one in particular, "let's go see what we can see." He walked to the farthest door in a tall building full of shops. I looked up and there they were again, threads skimming over the top of the building. Violet, green, orange. Even here I could see my way somewhere. Even if I couldn't get there on my own. Toy Man opened a glass door and stepped inside with me. Beyond the door was a cavernous entryway. The ceiling looked as if it might be as tall inside as Charity Birds. The walls were dazzling and painted in the same kingfisher blue as the walls of the hospital corridor, but they were interspersed with white shapes in a pattern made of all sharp edges and straight lines. I didn't think I'd ever seen anything like it! I sat on Toy Man's shoulder and pressed myself into his neck as he walked up to a counter.

"One ticket please," said Toy Man to a younger man seated at the desk. "How much is it?" Toy Man asked tentatively.

"Six hundred fifty rupees," said the younger man. He barely looked at Toy Man at all, and instead flicked his finger methodically along the smooth surface of a little device sitting on his desk. Toy Man carefully counted out his money and placed it on the desk and the younger man passed him a paper ticket.

"I'd like to bring in my bird." Toy Man reached a hand up to me and brushed his fingers along the feathers of my Only Wing. "She's very tame and she won't cause any trouble," he said. The younger man shrugged and waved us past his desk toward a door leading deeper into the building.

"Where do you think we are going, little kabootar?" Toy Man whispered to me as we passed into the first room. I flapped my Only Wing when I looked around and saw a rickshaw trapped on the ceiling, inverted as if it was about to fall. "It's OK, it's OK," said Toy Man, "this is only an illusion." He had a paper map unfolded in his hands and was turning it around in search of something in particular. "Yes," he said as he wandered through the rooms, "this is where we want to go." I had turned my face toward his hair. We were inside a place that I couldn't trust. The walls folded strangely and the sizes of everything inside shifted. It wasn't like the hospital, with its orderly corridor, the seeds and fruit at the same time each day, and the cooing of other birds.

When I felt Toy Man stop walking, I opened my eyes. We were in a room by ourselves. The walls were mirrors. Smooth and angled, and they reflected Toy Man and me back to ourselves over and over in rows. In the center of the room was a wide pedestal, with all kinds of different mirrors standing on it at strange angles. He lifted me from his shoulder and held me in both of his hands in front of a spot on the pedestal, and offered me up to my own reflection.

"Look, kabootar," he said. "Look at this. This is what could be. This is what you will become again someday." He had chosen a particular spot and turned me so that the side with my Only Wing was mirrored against itself. It was a wonderful trick. The reflection I saw was myself as I had been before the Kite Festival. Whole. The bird that looked back at me was on her own. Toy Man had stepped away from the mirror and out of the reflection. The mirror bird seemed to be out of place inside this building and this room. As though the only place she belonged was home, in the sky. "There's one more place I will take you," said Toy Man as he gently tucked me back into his bag.

Again, the noise of a station. A change in the quality of the air, the mechanical noises of metal hitting metal as trains slid into the station, swallowed a stream of passengers, and pushed their way out again. I heard everything through the fabric of Toy Man's bag. I felt nothing but the gentle pressure of his arm around me. When we were seated on the first train, Toy Man lifted me out of his bag and held me up to the window.

"Look, little kabootar," he said, placing a finger on the glass where he wanted me to see. "That is the Yamuna River. Right outside our city. You will fly there soon when you are well." Outside the window stretched a long and winding watery body. The surface was silky and dark and the banks rolled down gently to the water. Plants and trees and closely gathered bushes flourished everywhere. I thought that maybe it was where the kingfishers lived. And someday I could go there to see the same color as the walls of Charity Birds sail through the air. But then I remembered my wounded wing and how I wouldn't be able to get there on my own. We changed trains at an interchange station and the next train was too far from the river for me to see it from the window. But for the whole ride, Toy Man reminded me that it was there, calling for me.

When the voice in the train announced a stop for the Botanic Garden, Toy Man became suddenly animated.

"This is for us, kabootar!" He gathered me up and we rushed off the train, out of the station, and down to a walkway. Perched on his shoulder I watched as we passed a cluster of rickshaws. When I looked up, I saw the elevated track of the train looming over us. I knew that the curve of the track led all the way back to Old Delhi, and the market, and Charity Birds. It was like an enormous and imposing homing line. I could see that now. I wanted Toy Man to look too, but I didn't know how to tell him. And he was in a hurry. He kept waving away the rickshaw drivers offering him rides, and instead he quickened his steps down a walking path.

"Here we are, kabootar!" Toy Man was out of breath. He had pulled a white handkerchief from his bag, folded it into a tidy square and was dabbing at his forehead with it. "This is the Botanic Garden. This is the last place I wanted you to see today. Let's go in." He opened a black metal gate and walked through. I saw the vast expanse of green spread out before us, neatly trimmed hedges bordering the grass, and flowers blooming along the path. The metro track sailed above it all.

Toy Man sat down on a bench and set his bag next to him. I stayed on his shoulder as he rummaged around looking for something. After a few minutes he pulled out a handful of small odds and ends and little bits of discarded things and started fiddling with them making little toys the same way he did for me at Charity Birds. Toy Man didn't seem to notice anything around him as he assembled. But I saw a small girl standing on the path in front of him, her eyes wide as she watched him put together a pinwheel, like the one he had made for me. And then it wasn't just the girl there, but a small boy. And then two more girls, and then a slightly bigger boy. And then Toy Man finally looked up to see them all watching him. Saying nothing, he took a little propeller on a straw that he had made, spun it between his palms, and sent it flying up into the air toward the children. Toy Man began laughing with glee, as though this toy that he must have made many times before was as new to him as it was to all of them. And then they rushed toward him almost all at once. *Can you make it for me? What is that? Why is it flying? How do you make it play music?* And then, unexpectedly, *Is that your bird?*

Toy Man turned to look at me. "This little kabootar? Does she belong to me?"

The smallest boy nodded solemnly.

"She doesn't belong to me, beta. She doesn't belong to anyone but God. But I am taking care of her today," said Toy Man. "I want her to have a nice day. Like I want you to have a nice day too." Toy Man smiled and looked down to reknot a string that had broken.

"What happened to her wing?" the smallest girl asked.

"Kyaa beti?" Toy Man looked up and searched for the little girl's face.

"Why is her wing wrapped up?" The child pointed at me and I looked at my own wing. I had forgotten about the bandage today. I had forgotten that my wing hurt. The only thing I had not forgotten is that I cannot fly.

"She was hurt, beti. It's wrapped so she can heal."

"Can she fly?"

"Not yet, but she will." Toy Man looked over at me. I was perched on the back of the bench and had been walking back and forth along it so I could see the children and what Toy Man was making. He reached out his hand and I stepped onto it without even thinking. "She needs to remember what it was like to be in the sky."

But as I gripped onto the fabric of Toy Man's kurta on his shoulder, and he ran through the garden, I remembered something of the feeling of flying. I stretched out my Only Wing and felt the air move through my feathers. He was not fast. Toy Man is also an old man. But I was closer to being in the sky now. I felt as though I could reach my homing lines again. They were bright and luminous and they surrounded me. These running seams that stitch the city and the world together. I stretched my Only Wing out further. And this was almost like flying.

We took the metro back to the hospital as the day waned. To all the other passengers, Toy Man was merely an old man with a bird that they barely noticed. On every train we heard murmurs of *here, Uncle, take this seat. Here Uncle, there is space by this window.* I stayed on his shoulder at first, but as the journey

171

wore on, I hopped down into his lap to nestle in the crook of his elbow. The fabric of his clothing was worn soft. I caught myself cooing once or twice, drifting off to sleep to the rhythm of the train. And then we arrived at Chandni Chowk and Toy Man tucked me back into his bag as we left the train to return to the familiar sounds and smells of Old Delhi.

Toy Man let me sit on his shoulder as we walked back toward Charity Birds. As we made our way toward the red building, the sky was shot through with flames of color signaling the closing of the day. The lines glowed in incandescent orange as they ran like threads all pointing toward the hospital from every part of the city. I hadn't realized that the hospital had become marked this way on the map I held inside me. But here it was, my body and my eyes pulling me to return there. I wondered what it was like for Toy Man, who had never said anything about the lines to me and perhaps could not see them. As we got closer, I saw that Dr. Shah stood at the entrance, right outside the door in the courtyard. Her arms were crossed and she leaned against a pillar. Her white coat made her glow against the cooling light of the evening.

"Beti, I'm sorry," Toy Man began.

"Stop. Just stop." Dr. Shah held up her palm, but didn't move. "Uncle, I told you not to take her out today. Her wing is still healing and she needs to stay here."

"Yes, but—"

"Uncle," Dr. Shah pressed her fingers to her forehead, the same way I had seen her do after a long day. "I know you are trying to help. And we love having you come see us. Please understand that we are grateful. But taking an injured bird out is irresponsible. If you won't listen to me, then maybe it's better if you don't come for a while."

Toy Man had stopped walking. From where I was nestled on his shoulder, I could feel something in his body give way. A breath was exhaled, and with it, the wonder that had carried us through the day. He reached up and I felt his hand carefully scoop me from my perch. He held me in both of his hands and looked down at me. His eyes brightened like in the mirror room at the museum. And then he reached forward and held me out to her, as though I was an offering.

"I'm sorry, Dr. Shah," he said. "Yes, if you think it's best, I won't come anymore." He placed me in her hands gently. "Remember," he said, only to me, but perhaps also to her, "everything is going to be all right. Someday you will fly on your own to the river. Don't worry." I looked up at her. Her mouth was saying nothing. But her eyes were speaking about some sort of sadness. Above them both, the lines twisted and danced, unable to decide if the man, or the woman, or the building was meant to be home.

"Good-bye, Uncle, take care of yourself," Dr. Shah said. And then she brought me back inside and placed me in my cage. The orderly rows of the corridor, which I had missed all day, seemed somehow smaller now. I looked at my seed pile and my fruit, and I listened to the whirring of the fans, and I thought that perhaps it wasn't going to be enough for me. I wanted more than my Only Wing.

Toy Man didn't come back again to see me. But every day, when Dr. Shah took me out of my cage to examine me, I looked for him. Sometimes she would let me walk around on the floor in the corridor, or keep her company on the windowsill by her exam table as she cared for more urgent patients. I began stretching and moving my wounded wing more and more each day until it didn't really feel wounded anymore.

"Remarkable," Dr. Shah said one day as I stood on the sill and stretched both my wings out to feel the breeze drifting. "I didn't think this bird would recover that well." She was speaking to an assistant who was organizing supplies nearby.

"Of course she recovered, Dr. Shah," said her assistant. "Your care has been exceptional."

"I think we can take you to the roof soon," she said as she leaned toward me. "I think you're ready to return home."

That evening, I sat in my cage and I thought about home. It seemed as though it had been another, different bird who had spent the day out with Toy Man. And yet when Dr. Shah mentioned the roof, he became the only thing I could think about. Toy Man and the mirror illusion. Toy Man on the train. Toy Man showing me I could fly at the Botanic Garden. Toy Man and I traveling over the river. The river!

"I'm going to fly to the Yamuna," I said, more to myself than anything else.

"You aren't going to fly there," said the parakeet above me. "You'll fly to the market. Or maybe as far as the cricket field. But you're a pigeon. You aren't going to the river."

"I am," I said, entirely to myself.

Three days later Dr. Shah held me in her hands on the uppermost floor of Charity Birds Hospital.

"This is as far as I can go with you, little bird," she said. She stood on a staircase that led to the roof of the building. Over the opening of the staircase was a cage and at the top of the cage was a gap that led home, to the sky. "The rest of the way you will have to travel by yourself." I turned to look at her. Her dark hair was tucked back behind her ears and I remembered suddenly how the curtain of it had concealed me that first day. And how her hands had always felt warm and comforting. And how because of her, I had met Toy Man. And because of her, Toy Man had gone away. And because of Toy Man, I wanted to fly again. As I looked at her, and wished that I could tell her each of these things, I felt a feeling that I had not had since before the Kite Festival. A rising up inside of me. A feeling that I stood on a precipice, and that if I were to send myself over it, the wind would catch me. The sky would catch me. And I would be lifted to where I belong.

Dr. Shah put me down on the topmost step. I walked a few steps into the expanse of the cage. I flapped my wings a few times to test them. And then I lifted myself into the air and emerged from the top of the cage in a burst of color, my homing lines fully alive again. I circled over the building, and I looked at Charity Birds and at the market. I circled wider and could see the first metro station. And then I turned in the wind, found the violet thread, and flew toward the river.

AUTHOR'S NOTE

Sometimes I wonder whether I am wild, or I am tame. And then I remember it depends on who is answering that question. Consider, for instance, the birds in my neighborhood. There are a handful of undeveloped fields near my home that are filled with tall grass and ground squirrels. A few years ago, as I strolled past one on a midday walk, I heard urgent chirping. I looked down and saw an earth-toned bird about the size of a mourning dove staring at me defiantly with her wings spread out to her sides. Immediately behind her was her ground nest, and nestled inside were her eggs. As I walked by her, she turned her head to keep staring at me. She quieted her chirping only when I was a safe distance away. She was wild, and I am, in my own mind, tame. But am I? When I consider that day now, I imagine that she would say I am a predator. I stomped by with a relatively enormous head and giant clomping feet, and if I had decided to turn in to the field, I would have crushed her nest.

There is another bird that I think of often. Some years ago, I was on a family visit to a zoo and we all stood at an exhibit watching cheetahs, which are, in pretty much everyone's opinion, extremely glamorous. My husband tapped my shoulder and pointed out an exhibit opposite the cheetahs, just across the path. Inside, right up against the mesh of the cage, stood a tall bird with a majestic black crest. And he was staring at us. Watching us watch the cheetahs. I had come there as a spectator, but there I was, suddenly being observed. To me, he looked lonely, though there was no way I could communicate with him to understand whether that was true. I wondered whether he was traditionally a flocking bird, and whether life in that cage by himself left him so desolate that crowds of people staring at him was the closest he could feel to being among his own kind. And who was wild and who was tame in this scenario? Is he tame because of a life in captivity, and am I wilder because compared to him I am free? Perhaps we are both tame, because we both live in a world where our primary interaction is to watch each other.

I think also of my pets. All the pets I have had over my lifetime, and most importantly, the two cats in my home that were my dependable friends over the years that I wrote this collection. Every person who has ever lived with a cat will probably agree that it's not possible to own a cat, but it's very possible to befriend one. Over the years that we lived together, we developed a language of sorts; a way of communicating. So, when I call my cat's name, and she stays put and does not come trotting toward me humming that sweet amalgam between a purr and a meow, I know it's not because she doesn't know her own name. It's because she is choosing to ignore me. In this scenario, I think it is me that is tame.

If I were to set aside the traditional meanings of wildness and tameness and define them for myself, I would frame them in terms of dependence and communication. I imagine that for two living things (human or not), to be wild from each other is to have no need to communicate. But once the need to communicate arises, it breeds interaction, which creates interdependence, which creates more interaction, which requires more communication, which in my mind is how we tame each other.

I thought about all of this as I wrote these stories. Each time, I considered whether the animal whose story I told had any sort of need to communicate with humans. And if they did, what did they want from that communication? In some cases, humanity sat on the edge of the narrative, and though their influence was palpable, it was indirect. In these stories, I focused on which animals needed to communicate with each other, and why. In others, there was a direct relationship between my main animal character and a human. In these scenarios, I asked myself how much they depended on each other and imagined that the greater the interdependence, the greater their ability to communicate. For instance, in "Let Your Body Meet the Ground," the pigeon narrator is dependent upon Dr. Shah and Toy Man for her care and well-being, so it's important for her to understand them in order to comprehend what is happening to her. But they are not similarly dependent upon her, so they have less of a need to understand her. But, in "The Good Donkey," Hafiz and his donkey are surrogate family members to each other. They offer consistency and comfort to each other in a life turned upside down. They are interdependent both in a practical sense, and emotionally, and they needed to speak to each other without any limits.

Thinking about the ways my narrators did or did not interact with the humans around them helped me frame what features of our lives and world they might be familiar with and what would be incomprehensible. And it helped me re-envision how the environment looks when I distance myself from my own human perspective. How would a wolf describe a truck or a gun if she's never seen one before? How would a bird who's never left the city she lives in describe an elevated rail line? What does a devastating cyclone feel like to a tiger? What does the noise of a container ship do to the underwater world of a blue whale?

What helped me find my way to my own answers to these questions was to place myself inside the lives of my narrators by learning as much as I could about their environments and their behaviors, and imagining a fully realized self and life for each one. This was my first and most important inspiration for writing this collection. Every time I have learned about a different animal, I have wondered what they think about the world they live in. But the inner lives of animals are such a mystery to me, which has made me feel that my understanding of the world is incomplete. I am writing to fill that empty space for myself. In the end I did what I hope my readers will do: I dissolved the distance in my mind between myself and the wild world, which helped me understand that the story of my life includes the story of all the life that surrounds us.

Talia Lakshmi Kolluri

ACKNOWLEDGMENTS

The stories in this book have appeared in earlier form, or are forthcoming, in the following journals and magazines:

"The Good Donkey": *The Common* Issue 21

"What We Fed to the Manticore": *Ecotone* Issue 21

"Someone Must Watch Over the Dead": *Southern Humanities Review* Volume 55.3

"The Dog Star Is the Brightest Star in the Sky": *Five Dials* Summer 23 Issue

"The Hunted, the Haunted, the Hungry, the Tame": *The Minnesota Review* Issue 85

"A Level of Tolerance": *Southern Humanities Review* Volume 52.2

I wrote these stories over the long stretch of a little more than a decade, and I've been lucky to have the support of so many wonderful people.

To Kerry D'Agostino, thank you for understanding and supporting my creative vision, for always advocating for me, and for being the most compassionate guide through the process of sharing my book with the world. And thank you to everyone at Curtis Brown, Ltd. for your enthusiastic support.

The Tin House Summer Workshop is a rare and wonderful place, and I am so glad that Lance Cleland agreed to let me come and study there multiple times. Endless gratitude to my workshop classmates and their thoughtful reading of every story I brought to them. Thank you as well to the teachers who encouraged me to go wherever my imagination led me: Lan Samantha Chang, Anthony Doerr, and Claire Vaye Watkins.

Some of these stories appeared in literary journals in earlier forms and I am indebted to the editors and submissions queue readers who chose to take a chance on me. In particular, thank you to Beth Staples, Caitlin Rae Taylor, and Jennifer Acker for your thoughtful edits and for pushing me to be a better writer.

I am absolutely delighted that my debut is with Tin House, the place that first warmly welcomed me into the writing community. Thank you to everyone at Tin House for enthusiastically embracing my cast of animal characters and for providing such a wonderful home for my first book. Thank you in particular to Craig Popelars, Nanci McCloskey, Becky Kraemer, Masie Cochran, Alyssa Ogi, Jakob Vala, Alex Gonzales, Sangi Lama, Lanesha Reagan, Amanda Grosgebauer Bernardi, and Alice Yang. Thank you to Conor O'Brien and Jill Twist for thoughtful copyedits and proofreading. Thank you to Diane Chonette for designing the best book cover I have ever seen and to Jen Bartel for sharing your exquisite art for the cover.

Thank you most especially to Elizabeth DeMeo, who is technically my editor, but in practice is something more like an orchestra conductor. I am so glad that you read one of my stories and understood that there was a symphony there, and that you gathered all my lines of music and showed me the way to make them into something whole and wonderful.

To Claire Comstock-Gay, Ayşe Papatya Bucak, Elena Passarello, Blair Braverman, and Aimee Nezhukumatathil, thank you a million times over for your generosity and support!

Thank you to all the wonderful writer friends I have made over the years who have encouraged me, offered advice, answered my endless questions, and welcomed me into a vast and sprawling literary community. I would not be writing these acknowledgments now without the support of friends too many to name who have reached out a hand to pull me up, and shared resources, wisdom, and jokes. Thank you in particular to the writers who generously provided crucial notes on the stories in this collection as I worked my way through many revisions: Claire Comstock-Gay, Lisa Michelle Jackson, Jeni McFarland, Jocelyn Nicole Johnson, Melanie Nead, Rowan Hisayo Buchanan, Lara Prescott, Sujata Shekar, and Sharon Gelman.

Thank you to my hometown writing group: Carole Firstman, Jim Schmidt, Sally Vogl, and Ethan Chatagnier for inspiring me to take risks, and for providing essential guidance as I finished this collection. Thank you also to Ethan for always being generous with your time, your advice, and your encouragement.

Thank you to the many science and nature writers whose work I devoured, and who made it easy for me to climb inside the hearts and minds of the animals I was curious about.

Thank you to my friends, neighbors, and community for encouraging me for so many years, and for celebrating even the smallest milestones with me.

A billion hugs for my wonderful family, all my beloved aunts, uncles, cousins, nieces and nephews, and my sister, all of whom enthusiastically cheered me on, even when nothing exciting was happening. And to my sister, Sonya, who taught me to play make-believe: whoops I guess I never stopped!

I am forever grateful to my wonderful husband, Jared Barbick, who believed that I would write a book before I even started, who has always found something to love in my work, who fed my imagination with his own art, and who persistently encouraged me to dream beyond the reach of my own hands.

My final thanks are for two beloved feline friends, Fig and (the late) Lulu. They neither speak nor read English, and don't have the thumbs needed to turn the pages of this book all the way to the acknowledgments. But without them I may never have learned to step outside myself far enough to see the world with wilder eyes.

SOURCES

THE GOOD DONKEY

"Bleak Outlook for Bombed Gaza Zoo," by Aleem Maqbool, BBC News, February 18, 2009, http://news.bbc.co.uk/2/hi/middle_east /7897385.stm.

The Drone Eats with Me: Diaries from a City under Fire, by Atef Abu Saif, published by Comma Press, 2015.

"Hamas Helps Release Another Gaza Hostage: A Lioness," by Matthew Weaver, *The Guardian* online, July 9, 2007, https://www .theguardian.com/world/2007/jul/09/israel.

"The Man Behind Gaza's Fake Zebras," by Mahmoud Barghout, *The Guardian* online, November 4, 2009, https://www.theguardian .com/world/2009/nov/04/gaza-zoology.

Palestinian Walks: Forays into a Vanishing Landscape, by Raja Shehadeh, published by Scribner, 2008.

WHAT WE FED TO THE MANTICORE

"Three Years after Cyclone, Changed Lives in Sundarbans," by Anuradha Sharma, *New York Times*, May 28, 2012, https://india

.blogs.nytimes.com/2012/05/28/three-years-after-cyclone-changed -lives-in-sundarbans.

"Tigers under Threat from Disappearing Mangrove Forest," by John Vidal, *The Guardian* online, January 29, 2013, https:// www.theguardian.com/environment/2013/jan/29/sunderbans -disappearing-mangrove-india-bangladesh.

SOMEONE MUST WATCH OVER THE DEAD

"Death in the City: How a Lack of Vultures Threatens Mumbai's 'Towers of Silence,'" by Bachi Karkaria, *The Guardian* online, January 26, 2015, https://www.theguardian.com/cities/2015/jan/26/death -city-lack-vultures-threatens-mumbai-towers-of-silence.

"Why Did Two-Thirds of These Weird Antelope Suddenly Drop Dead?" by Ed Yong, *The Atlantic* online, January 17, 2018, https:// www.theatlantic.com/science/archive/2018/01/why-did-two -thirds-of-this-weird-antelope-suddenly-drop-dead/550676.

THE DOG STAR IS THE BRIGHTEST STAR IN THE SKY

"Here Be White Bears," by Michael Engelhard, *Hakai Magazine*, May 30, 2017, https://hakaimagazine.com/features/here-be-white -bears.

"Melting Arctic Ice Is Forcing Polar Bears to Swim for More Than a Week without Rest," by Sarah Kaplan, *Washington Post*, April 21, 2016, https://www.washingtonpost.com/news/speaking-of-science/wp /2016/04/21/melting-arctic-ice-is-forcing-polar-bears-to-swim-for -more-than-a-week-without-rest.

MAY GOD FOREVER BLESS THE RHINO KEEPERS

"At Home with the World's Last Male Northern White Rhinoceros," by Murithi Mutiga in *Ol Pejeta*, *The Guardian* online, April 27, 2015, https://www.theguardian.com/environment/2015/apr/27/ol-pejeta -kenya-sudan-worlds-last-male-northern-white-rhinoceros.

"Seeing Spirituality in Chimpanzees," by Barbara J. King, *The Atlantic* online, March 29, 2016, https://www.theatlantic.com/science/archive /2016/03/chimpanzee-spirituality/475731.

THE HUNTED, THE HAUNTED, THE HUNGRY, THE TAME

"The Cold Patrol," by Michael Finkel (photos by Fritz Hoffman), *National Geographic Magazine*, January 2012, https://www .nationalgeographic.com/magazine/article/cold-patrol.

Dogs on the Trail: A Year in the Life, by Blair Braverman and Quince Mountain, published by Ecco, 2021.

THE OPEN OCEAN IS AN ENDLESS DESERT

"The Blue Whale's Heart Beats at Extremes," by Ed Yong, *The Atlantic* online, November 25, 2019, https://www.theatlantic.com/science /archive/2019/11/diving-blue-whales-heart-beats-very-very-slowly /602557.

The Breath of the Whale: the Science and Spirit of Pacific Ocean Giants, by Leigh Calvez, published by Sasquatch Books, 2019.

A LEVEL OF TOLERANCE

"The Death of 832F, Yellowstone's Most Famous Wolf," by Jeff Hull, *Outside* online, February 13, 2013, https://www.outsideonline.com/outdoor-adventure/environment/out-bounds-death-832f-yellowstones-most-famous-wolf.

"'Famous' Wolf Is Killed outside Yellowstone," by Nate Schweber, *New York Times* online, December 8, 2012, https://www.nytimes.com/2012/12/09/science/earth/famous-wolf-is-killed-outside-yellowstone.html.

The Hidden Lives of Wolves, by Jim Dutcher and Jamie Dutcher with James Manful, published by the National Geographic Society, 2013.

White Wolf, directed by Jim Brandenburg.

The Wisdom of Wolves, by Jim Dutcher and Jamie Dutcher with James Manful, published by National Geographic Partners, LLC, 2018.

Wolves: Behavior, Ecology, and Conservation, ed. L. David Mech and Luigi Boitani, published by University of Chicago Press, 2003.

LET YOUR BODY MEET THE GROUND

The Genius of Birds, by Jennifer Ackerman, published by Penguin Books, 2016.

"A Journey into the Animal Mind: What Science Can Tell Us about How Other Creatures Experience the World," by Ross Andersen, *The Atlantic*, March 2019, https://www.theatlantic.com/magazine/archive/2019/03/what-the-crow-knows/580726.

"#LBBPhotoStory: This Hospital Believes Birds Should Fly Free & We Agree," by Siddhi Soi, undated, https://lbb.in/delhi/charity-bird -hospital-jain-mandir.

"Turning Trash into Toys for Learning," Arvind Gupta, TED Talk, December 2010, https://www.ted.com/talks/arvind_gupta_turning _trash_into_toys_for_learning?language=en.

PHOTO © SARAH DERAGON

TALIA LAKSHMI KOLLURI's short fiction has appeared in *The Minnesota Review, Ecotone, Southern Humanities Review, The Common,* and elsewhere. She was born and raised in Northern California and currently lives in California's beautiful Central Valley with her husband and cat.